DEMON'S DESTINY

GUARDIANS

VALERIE TWOMBLY

Copyright © 2015 by Valerie Twombly

Editing by: JRT Editing

Cover by: Original Syn

All rights reserved.

No part of this book may be reproduced in any form or by any electronic or mechanical means, including information storage and retrieval systems, without written permission from the author, except for the use of brief quotations in a book review.

ISBN: 978-1-7326306-7-3

2nd Edition

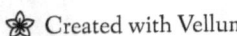 Created with Vellum

CHAPTER ONE

BAAL HAD NEVER BEEN TURNED down before. Not once. Ever. He stared at the woman behind the bar who had so much as refused to even give him her name. He'd closed the place down a couple of nights ago with Seth, or had it been longer? He couldn't remember after taking a couple of those damn pills. Either way, he did remember craving a piece of the vision currently giving him the evil eye. Still did. He hadn't come across a female like her in a long time.

"Seriously, why are you working in this shit hole? You should be strutting your stuff in designer clothes and high heels." Black hair curled around her shoulders, blue, almond-shaped eyes were fringed with thick lashes, add to that high cheekbones and pouty lips and you had exotic perfection. Not to mention the curves he wanted to sink his fingers into while he fucked the hell out of her.

She laughed. "I suppose you're going to promise me a starring role in your next movie?"

He reached into his jacket pocket and pulled out a card. "Nope, but I need a hostess for my casino." He tossed the card on the bar. She rolled her eyes then threw her towel aside and picked up the card.

"Dragon's Cove?" She eyed him suspiciously. "I've heard of it." She snorted and tossed it back on the bar. "Right, and I suppose you're gonna tell me you own the place?"

He shrugged. "Okay, I won't tell you that, but I do."

"Please, I'm not that stupid. Why would someone who owned a highly successful Vegas club be here in—as you called it—this shit hole?"

"I came to help a friend who was down and out."

She reached for a dirty glass and ran it through the washer. "The dark-haired guy? He seemed like he'd seen better days."

"He has, but I think things will be improving for him soon. Now back to my offer. I was serious when I said I need someone. You think about it and if you'd like I'll fly you in for an interview and to talk terms."

She wiped her hands and picked up the card again. Stared at it while pulling her bottom lip through her teeth. He could almost see the smoke coming out her ears. "I don't get it. Vegas has to be full of people who qualify for the job. What do you want from me?"

No way in hell could he tell her what he really wanted was to strip her, toss her on top of the bar and taste every inch of her. He'd have to work his way up to that one. "You desire more than this, I can tell." No lie there. The ability to read a human's desire was bred into every demon. It's how the evil spread, some chose to use it for bad and others good. In this case his intentions were for a little of both. "Your beauty shouldn't be wasted here."

"I've always wanted to leave, but have never had the means to do so."

"Well, this is your chance." He tipped back the last swill of his beer and set the glass on the bar. "I have to leave and head back. You can Google me all night long and see that I'm who I say. Call that number and I will send a limo and my private jet to pick you up. You can have a room in the hotel. I promise, no strings attached." His charm and demon good looks would bewitch the pants right off her. He just needed the chance.

"I'll think about it." She tucked the card into her back pocket and suddenly he was jealous of the tiny piece of glossy paper.

He tipped his head. "Fair enough." Then headed for the door.

"Wait!"

He stopped dead in his tracks and held his breath. Had she changed her mind already? "Yes?" he asked and turned slowly.

"My name, it's Ranata."

"Beautiful name." He pulled open the door and stepped into the cool night air. Took a deep breath and scanned for any humans before he flashed.

RANATA SHOOK her head as she watched the man walk out of the bar. She might consider his offer, except she needed to find her sister. Raven hadn't returned her calls in over two weeks, and Ranata was worried sick. She suspected her younger sibling had gotten mixed up in some cult activity. When she'd searched Raven's room for clues, she'd found things that scared the shit out of her. Books on devil worship were hidden under her sister's mattress. Then there was Clive, the jerk Raven had taken to hanging out with. Most people would be scared of him solely due to his tattoos and piercings. However, Ranata didn't judge people on how they looked. No, there was something inside him that gave her the creeps. She just couldn't put her finger on it.

She washed the last of the glasses and finished cleaning off the bar then headed to lock the front door. With a quick glance around to make sure everything was in place, she made her way to the back room. The cook had left half an hour ago, so she was the last one to close up the place. After grabbing her purse, she stepped out the back door and into the dim light, making a mental note to ask the owner to change out the old, fading light bulb. She hated closing up alone, and walking across the dark, gravel parking lot at three in the morning made her hair stand on end.

Halfway to her car, she got the distinct feeling of being watched. She picked up the pace and prayed it was only her imagination freaking her out. The relief she experienced when she grabbed the car door handle was short-lived. An arm snaked around her waist and jerked her backward.

She screamed.

A large hand slapped over her mouth. "Bitch, you should have minded your own business and left things alone."

She recognized Clive's gruff voice and tried to jerk herself free while raising her foot and giving a swift kick behind her.

She made contact with his knee.

"Fucking shit! You're gonna pay for that." His hand moved from her mouth to around her neck and squeezed. He spun her to face him and slapped her across the cheek. A coppery taste coated her tongue. "You're fucking lucky they want you to stay scar-free, or I'd bash in that pretty little face of yours."

Ranata tried to claw at him, but he shoved her against the car and pinned her arms between them. "Though I doubt they'd care if I had a piece of you before I hand you over." He loosened his grip around her neck then grabbed the collar of her tee and ripped it down the middle.

She spit in his face, managed to free one hand and clawed at his cheek. Clive let loose, and she ran screaming across the parking lot. The chance of anyone hearing her was nil since the bar was located in the middle of nowhere. Her best bet was to head for the woods and pray she could lose him in the thick brush.

Her lungs burned as she gasped for air and headed for the tree line. She scurried into the thicket, tripping over something. She went down with a hard thud. Before she could get up, someone grabbed her ankles and dragged her backward. She screamed and clawed at the ground. Bile gagged her at the thought of what Clive would do to her now.

"You little fucking slut!" He was on top of her and jerked her jeans past her hips. "You should have just played nice and taken what's coming to you. Now, I don't give a shit what condition I deliver you in."

Her heart beat wildly as she tried to calm herself enough to form a plan. "Clive, don't do this. Think about Raven and what this will do to her." She hoped to appeal to any scrap of humanity he had.

He laughed. "I don't give two shits about your sister. She's served her purpose, and now, I'll have you then hand you over to the devil himself." He tried to kiss her, and she bit his lip.

He hit her so hard her ears rang. She knew there was no way to win against him, but she'd die fighting. Just as he ripped her panties, he was jerked off her.

"Really, Clive?"

Ranata scrambled to grab her jeans and jerked them back on. "Oh, thank god, Father." She'd never been so happy to see the church's priest, Father Ryan, in her life.

He shoved Clive to the side and reached his hand out. "Are you all right?"

She gladly accepted, and he helped her to her feet, but as happy as she was to see him, she had to wonder what he was doing out here. When she felt a needle sink into her arm, shock filled her.

"Sorry, Ranata, but I need you to placate the devil," Father Ryan whispered.

"Wha— B-but I don't understand." Whatever was in that syringe had already begun to work. Darkness swirled in her head, and there was nothing she could do to stop it.

"THIS IS LIKE OLD TIMES, my friend." Baal settled in for a long wait with his friend Marcus. The guardian next to him was as lethal as any, but also a healer. It was a rare gift among their kind that had come in handy on several occasions. Hopefully, they would not be in need of such skills tonight.

Planted in a spot deep in the forest of the Black Hills. The location was remote and had all the indications of being a sacrificial ground used by devil worshippers. Baal shrouded them in magic so they could get a close-up view without being detected.

"Sorry, but you are not who I wanted to spend my evening with." Marcus ran a cloth over his dagger, polishing it to such a high sheen the moonlight reflected off it and nearly blinded Baal.

"Well, I can't say I blame you. Hell, I'd rather spend time with Cassie than your sorry ass, too."

Marcus flashed the blade under the demon's nose. "Careful, old friend. You know how I get about my mate."

Baal snorted. He knew first-hand and had seen the vampire's fangs on several occasions when Marcus had hissed out warnings to other males. Baal couldn't blame the man, though. Marcus had been to hell and back and seen more heartache than any man should. Baal was glad the guardian had finally found happiness. It had improved his mood immensely, as well.

"What about you?"

Baal flashed a glance at the vampire. "Me what?"

"Do you wish for stability? A mate? Children?"

The demon clutched his gut and tried not to laugh. "I thought you knew me better. I'm allergic to being with one woman." He shuddered. "I break out in hives at the thought." There was a time when he would have given anything to have those things. Instead, the gods had ripped his heart out and ground it under their heels. It was then he'd vowed he'd never love again. Ever.

Marcus laughed. "One of these days a female will chop your balls off."

"A few have tried. Unsuccessfully, I might add." Though he'd never admit it out loud, there had been a couple of close calls. Yeah, human women didn't much care for sharing their men, so he mostly stuck to the immortal variety. They could care less and were happy to share in a good time until their mate came along. He inhaled. "I smell humans."

"Ditto. I'd say the show is about to start," Marcus replied.

They didn't have long to wait before several people appeared in the clearing. All of them wore hooded, black robes. The one in front carried a tall staff with a skull on the top. It was evident he was the leader. Another shoved a young female, dressed in a white gown with a black sack over her head, toward the front. Both warriors stiffened.

"I don't like the looks of this." Marcus pulled a second dagger from his boot.

"Neither do I. It seems as though they plan a human sacrifice." Baal freed his own blade. "We can't simply rush in there, or we'll break our cover."

The guardian pinned him with a lethal glare. "Then you'd best come up with a plan and fast. I cannot sit here and watch them kill her." He looked back at the gathering crowd, his lips in a thin line. "I, more than anyone, want to find Lowan, but not at the expense of a human's life."

"It's possible she volunteered."

"Don't give a fuck," Marcus snarled, his fangs extending.

"Okay, I'll go in if I have to, but let's see what they're up to first."

Twenty people gathered around the one who carried the staff and grew deadly silent. The girl was dragged to a makeshift altar while she tried to fight off her captors. *Okay, so much for her volunteering.*

"Brothers and sisters. Tonight, I am pleased to tell you that our god has finally answered our call," the leader spoke out. "He has sent his own grandson to guide us and show us the way."

Baal rolled his eyes, knowing damn well that Hades hadn't sent Lowan to the human realm. *Stupid humans.*

Whispers grew among the crowd. Some questioned the validity of the one who carried the staff but kept their tones hushed enough that only Baal and Marcus heard them.

"Tonight, all our brethren across the world will show their thanks by offering the blood of a human female. Let this moment mark the coming of the darkness."

The others chanted in Latin as they tied the struggling girl to the altar.

"Baal, now would be a good time for your plan." Panic edged Marcus's voice.

The demon smiled. "Watch this." He flashed then reappeared at the foot of the altar. He'd shifted his form, so he had thick, black skin and red eyes. Two horns protruded from the top of his head and the top of his shoulders. He'd enlarged his small fangs until they would make even a vampire cringe.

The crowd stepped back, including the two who'd been heading toward the female, their fists wrapped around the daggers meant to bleed her.

"Release the female." Baal lowered his voice several octaves until it was a low rumble.

The gang dropped to their knees, including the one who had led the clan to the stone slab. He was the first to speak.

"M-my lord, doesn't the female please you?"

"She will please me more alive." He sensed the woman's heart rate increase. Hell, he scared her as much as the assholes in front of him had.

"Of course, whatever you wish." The leader snapped his fingers at the two goons in front. "Untie her." They scrambled to do his bidding and pulled the female from the altar, dragging her to Baal.

"Now, leave us so I may enjoy her at my leisure."

The people jumped to their feet and scurried away. Baal detected the sounds of car doors being slammed and engines revved as they squealed out of sight. Before he could react, the girl ripped off her hood, screamed at him and took off on a dead run. Shit, he'd forgotten to shift back, and now that she was untied, she had no trouble escaping into the darkness.

Marcus flashed next to him. "I'll fetch her and erase her memories."

"No. I'll get her. You wait here." Before he could move, demons attacked. Coming from all directions, they managed to take Marcus and Baal by surprise.

Baal produced a sword, swung and made contact with one head then a second as he spun on the ball of his foot. Marcus, with a dagger in each hand, used a crisscross action that took out two more. Both men spun and wielded their weapons, but the demons didn't relent.

A scream pierced the night's sky.

"Shit, the girl," Baal yelled.

"Go! I'll be right behind you."

Baal flashed, found himself behind a tree. Two demons came out of the darkness, straight at him. He summoned his magic and launched a fireball at each. It knocked them back, but they were only stunned. He tuned his senses and picked up a struggle ahead. He flashed again. This time hitting pay dirt. The woman fought with a lone slasher. The creature looked the part of pure evil with its taloned fingertips, rows of razor teeth and horn-lined shoulders and arms, but it was dumber than a box of rocks.

Baal whistled. "Hey, dumbshit." The beast turned to pin beady green eyes on him. "Yeah, I'm talking to you. Come get me, fucktard."

The demon lunged, but his seven-foot size made him slow. Baal produced his sword at the last second and decapitated the beast. The girl screamed and took off running again.

"Damn it, woman," he growled.

"We need to hurry and get out of here. There are more coming," Marcus yelled from behind him.

This time, Baal took off running, following the scent of fear, and in seconds, he was behind her. "Wait, I'm one of the good guys," he yelled.

The girl was apparently too terrified to register what he'd said so he flashed in front of her. She ran right into him, and he wrapped his arms around her slender, trembling frame.

"It's okay." He gripped her arms and pushed her back to get a look at her. Wild eyes looked up at him, and he was sure the color drained from his face. "Ranata, how the hell...?"

Marcus came up behind him. "We need to get out of here, like yesterday."

Baal nodded, pulled Ranata into him and flashed.

CHAPTER TWO

BAAL RUSHED through the compound the guardians had tucked away deep in a mountain. The Chosen, those select humans who knew about the immortals and assisted them with their dealings in the mortal world, were scattered around the area. Since Lowan had managed to find a way to free himself from his prison in Hell, and was currently creating havoc in the human world, everyone had come here to prepare for the worst.

He needed to find Ranata.

The desire to make sure she was unharmed slammed into him like a freight train. He hated that innocents were caught up in their war, and hoped she could tell him how she'd almost become a human sacrifice. He spotted Marcus leaving Seth's room.

"Where did they take the girl we rescued?"

Marcus halted. "She should be with the Chosen on the lower level."

That was somewhat of a relief. At least, she was with other humans. "Who will be guarding the compound when we all leave?"

"Aidyn has arranged for several Draki to stay behind."

Baal rubbed his chin. Having the dragons on guard was a wise move. "Good choice. I need to speak with the girl. I'll catch up with you later." He flashed to the lower level of the compound. People were parked at various tables in the large room, tapping furiously on the keys of their laptops. Some stared at the wall of monitors and whispered into headsets. Baal knew these were the worker bees who would keep their fingers on the pulse of what was going on. They had families, though, who must be stationed in another area, and most likely, that's where he'd find Ranata.

He scanned the room and spotted Daniel seated alone at a table. Baal sidled up beside him. "Where are the other humans?"

Daniel looked up from his computer. "They're spread out all over this wing. Who are you looking for?"

"The one who doesn't belong here."

"Ah. The dark-haired girl who looks like she's about to freak out at any minute?"

"Precisely."

"I believe they put her down the hall in a private room."

"Great, I'll find her." Baal spun on his heel and headed out of the room and into the corridor. He took a deep breath. Being a demon came in handy. He smelled fear better than any other immortal, and the strong, heady scent of it came from several doors down.

He snarled and moved toward it until he found himself standing outside a heavy door. She was on the other side, there was no doubt about it. None of the other humans in the compound would be this frightened as they were accustomed to dealing with the supernatural. He had to remind himself he was on the good side of the fight and to rein in his instinct to prey on people's fears. He was a demon, after all.

He rapped on the door. "Ranata?" Silence greeted him. It appeared she wouldn't answer, not that he blamed her. With a sigh, he jiggled the handle. Locked.

Damn it. He'd have to use his magic to open the door and probably terrify her further. "I'm coming in, so you best make sure you're decent." With a quick burst of power, he released the lock then pushed open the door.

Ranata greeted him with a scowl from the chair across the room. "Have you come to release me?" Her tone was anything but pleased.

"What? No thanks for saving you?"

Fear radiated from her and turned her aura an orange-yellow encased in black, yet she lifted her chin, pulled back her shoulders and tried to put on a brave front. "Thanks. Now, can I leave?"

She was a courageous woman, and that fascinated him even more. "It's not safe out there. That brings me to the question of how you ended up with those people."

"Are you my father now?"

He usually had a level temper, was even what they called easygoing, but this chick pushed his buttons. That pissed him off even more. "No, I'm not. I am, however, the one who saved your ass. Don't you realize what they were about to do to you?"

She shivered. Pulling her knees to her chest, she wrapped her arms around herself. "I do, and I'm sorry." Tears welled up in her blue eyes. "T-that thing they were going to sacrifice me to. It was the most horrible thing I've ever seen. When I saw those fangs, I nearly died from fright."

He fought the urge to blurt out that *he* was the beast she feared. Instead, he refrained. "You're safe now."

She nodded and sniffed. "I thought I could find my sister, but instead, I only got myself into trouble." A single drop slid down her cheek. "I'm afraid for her. What if those people sacrificed her? I need to find out, and I can't do it in here."

Well now, didn't he feel like a shithead? "I'm sorry about your sister. Come with me. I need to show you something."

She stood and walked toward him. He held out his hand, and she hesitated for a moment before accepting. The warmth that came over him when she slipped her hand in his, momentarily threw him off guard. He led her out the door and steered her along the same corridor he'd just come down and back to the hub of activity, where he pointed to the bank of monitors on the wall. "Have you seen the world news?"

She approached with caution and slipped into a vacant chair. Her eyes were glued to the TVs as the media showed the masses trying to exit the city in any fashion they could. Traffic had stopped, and people abandoned their cars and ran on foot. Humans were being trampled by their own or attacked by demons. Some were dragged off, screaming, while others were tortured in front of the cameras.

Baal fought to control his anger, lest he frighten Ranata more. His heart went out to all the innocents, and he itched to jump into the thick of things and start slicing through the evil. "It's not safe out there."

She looked up at him with terror-filled eyes. He wanted to scoop her up and tell her everything would be fine, but he didn't have a crystal ball. He wasn't even sure the gods knew what the outcome would be.

Her lip trembled. "My sister, she can't be dead. I'd know." She glanced around the room as if finally noticing her surroundings. "Where am I, and who are all these people?"

He sighed. "It's a rather long story, and one that will have to wait for another day. Just know that you are in one of the safest places in the world right now. As for your sister..." He couldn't believe what he was about to say. "I'll try to find her for you."

RANATA GLANCED at her surroundings then back to the man who stood in front of her. How the hell had she managed to get herself into such a mess? Everything was a bit blurry, and she wasn't sure she wanted to remember. What those men had planned for her... What Clive would have done to her if... She remembered Father Ryan. He'd saved her from one fate then condemned her to another.

She shivered.

"You chilled?" Baal asked.

She didn't know what she was, but one thing was certain. She didn't think she'd ever give her trust so easily again. Too many she'd trusted had already betrayed her. "No, but I want answers. Where am I, and how did you find me?"

The man gave a visible sigh. "Well, you'll find out sooner or later. This is headquarters for... Well, think of them as your guardian angels." He waved his hand. "These people are the humans who work for them."

His lips moved, but she didn't understand a word he said. "So... you're sayin' angels live here?" She looked around again but didn't see any wings. Only men and women who tapped on computers and spoke into cell phones.

"Well, they aren't exactly what you think. No wings, only fangs."

"Fangs. Huh." Moving on then. "So how did you find me?" When she'd run from her captors, she'd had no idea where she was but realized she'd been in the middle of nowhere.

He lifted a shoulder. "I was with my friend, Marcus, and we were scouting the area. I saw them getting ready to do you in."

She shivered again at the remembrance of removing her hood and seeing the large monster they'd intended to give her to. "I'm grateful beyond belief, but how are you involved in this?" She needed to know who and what she was dealing with. His eyes deepened to a hue so rich it reminded her of liquid gold. Never before had she seen such an exotic and beautiful color, yet something lay behind them. Secrets. She didn't know how or why she knew this.

He raised a black brow. "Why do you want to know?"

Yes, he was definitely hiding something. Why hadn't she noticed it earlier in the bar when he'd handed her his card and asked her to come to Vegas for a job? Ranata chocked it up to being distracted by his good looks. The fall of dark curls that touched the collar of his shirt and the light shadow along his jaw mesmerized her. She found herself wondering if shaving ever erased the darkness on his skin. Her gaze dropped to the black tee that hugged a hard body underneath.

For a moment, she was jealous of the lucky fabric but quickly regained composure.

"I like to know who I can trust." She looked back at the screens on the wall that still played the horror outside. It would be too easy to pretend she was watching the latest Stephen King flick, but she knew the truth. She'd landed right smack in the middle of Hell.

He opened his mouth then snapped it shut only to sigh. "Fine, I don't believe in lies. I'm a demon, and I'm here to help."

She blinked as if opening and closing her eyes would change what he'd said. He must have realized she was having a difficult time with his statement. He held out his hand with his palm open, and within seconds, a ball of fire the size of a grapefruit formed.

She gasped and took a step backward. "How'd you do that?"

"Magic."

Her skin prickled, as if she'd been plugged into an electrical circuit. Come to think of it, she'd been experiencing the same feeling since she'd been brought into this facility. The fireball shrank in size until it disappeared, and the so-called demon dropped his hand to his side.

"Why don't you look like the others?" she inquired.

"Because I choose not to, but I can change my form at any time."

The fact that he was a demon should put her on edge, but it didn't, and she questioned her sanity. "Are you a killer?" She stared back at the screens. "Like them?"

"Never. Not all demons are evil."

There were a million questions she wanted to ask, but another person approached. It was the same guy who had been drinking with Baal at the bar. He stopped and stared at her.

"You should be more careful of the company you keep," he stated.

"Your name was Seth. Right?" The man certainly looked better than the last time she'd seen him.

His blue gaze pinched down. "Yes, and I hear you were lucky Baal was around to save you. How the hell did you end up as a sacrifice?"

She shoved down her unstable emotions. "Look, I'm grateful for everything, but I'm not in the mood for fifty questions. Show me the exit, and I'll be on my way."

"Listen up, cupcake. You're not going anywhere. Didn't you learn anything from your experience?" Baal's sarcasm pushed all the wrong buttons.

Ranata dug her nails into her palms and tried to steady her breathing. *God, not now. Not here!* The caldron that was her stomach threatened to erupt. Sweat trickled down the back of her neck. *Why is this happening to me?* There was no stopping it this time, so she took off at a dead run back toward the room where she'd been previously.

BAAL WAS MOMENTARILY stunned when Ranata took off on a dead run. Did she think she would find a way out? He stormed after her and heard Seth laughing behind him.

"Fucking vampire," he mumbled under his breath. There was nothing amusing about the situation. Instead of busting some demon ass, he was busy babysitting. "What did I ever do to be punished in this manner?" It seemed as though he were forever looking after someone.

There was no rush on his part since she couldn't escape, plus he could scent her. She'd gone back to her room. *How convenient.*

"Running from me won't help," he yelled, stepping into the room. "And neither will locking the door." He stood in the center of the small living area and looked around. She was nowhere in sight then he heard it. The sound of someone retching. Concern carried him straight into the bathroom where he found her hugging the toilet.

"Ranata, are you ill?"

"How observant. Now, go away!" Her body trembled.

"Don't think so." He knelt next to her and pulled her hair from the side of her face, and it was then he noticed the tears. *Marcus, I need you to come check on the girl.* He hoped the guardian healer wasn't too far away. His telepathic link with Marcus didn't have long-distance service.

"Are you well enough to move? We need to get you to bed."

She didn't say a word but nodded, so he wasted no time scooping her up and headed for the bed. He was about to lay her down when Marcus flashed in.

"What's going on?"

Ranata stiffened in his arms.

"It's okay. I called him. Marcus is a healer, and I think he should take a look at you." Baal didn't wait for her to agree. "I found her hugging the toilet. Maybe, a case of the human flu?" He laid her down.

"Well, I can certainly fix that." Marcus sat on the edge of the mattress. "Do you mind if I touch you?"

She gave him a sideways look. "Touch me how?"

Marcus raised a brow. "Perhaps, you'd be more comfortable if my wife were here? She's a healer, too."

Relief swept over Ranata's features. "Yes. Yes, I think I would."

Seconds later, Cassie flashed into the room and exchanged places with her mate. "Hi, I'm Cassie." She stuck out her hand, and instantly, Ranata reached for it. Baal felt a sense of relief. He should have called Cassie in the first place.

"Nice to meet you."

"I understand you're not feeling well?" The female guardian flashed a warm smile.

"I... Actually, I'm feeling better now. It must be nerves."

"Well, I can certainly understand why. With all that's going on and what you've been through, it's no wonder." Cassie kept hold of Ranata's hand for a few more seconds before she let go.

"Wow. You did something to me. What was that?" Ranata made a move to sit up.

"I simply sent you a little healing energy, but you should rest if you can."

Ranata hugged her knees to her chest. "I want to leave. I need to find my sister."

"You're aware it's not safe out there?" Marcus approached and stood behind his wife.

Ranata tipped her head to look up at him. "I know that, but you can't keep me here."

Marcus sighed. "You're right, but I cannot spare the manpower to help you. The choice is yours, and of course, you're not a prisoner here."

"You can't seriously send her out into that shit. I just fucking rescued her!" Baal fought to keep his demon under control.

Marcus eyed him. "I cannot hold her against her will. She's a grown woman and fully aware of the situation."

Baal growled then checked himself. "Ranata. I said I would help locate your sister, but under one condition."

She lifted a dark brow, and her blue eyes sparked with fire. Damn, she was a feisty one. "Which would be?"

"I'll take you out of here and give you refuge in one of my homes, but you must promise you'll stay put while I look for your sister." Marcus and Cassie both glanced at him but kept quiet. Yeah, he was as surprised as they appeared to be.

"Why should I trust you?" She crossed her arms over her breasts, and he felt the loss of such a beautiful view.

"Because you have no choice, and it's a smart decision."

She pulled in a deep breath. "That's not an answer. I don't know you from Adam, and yet, you expect me to trust you?"

"I saved your life."

She rolled her eyes. "I'm not so stupid that I don't realize you've been trying to get into my pants since we first met."

"Won't deny it." There was no reason to lie since she was correct. "However, that was before. I have every intention of helping you find your sister."

Her brows pinched down. "So, now you're saying you don't have any sexual intentions?"

Damn. Did he still? Well, she was one hot number, but even he wouldn't stoop that low. "I'm not going to lie. You're a beautiful woman, but I'm not a creep. I don't force myself on anyone. Consent must be mutual. And... Well, shit has changed." He scratched his head. "There are more important things that need our attention."

She studied him for a long moment, looking as if she were gauging the truthfulness of his statement. "Fine."

"Say it." He didn't know why, but he needed the words from her lips.

"Say what?" She squinted at him.

"Give me your promise."

"Fine. I promise I'll stay in your home." She leaned forward. "But you must also promise I'll be safe, and that includes from you, as well."

"I give my word." He couldn't believe he'd just made a pact with her. Why the hell hadn't he left the girl here and walked away?

She gave Cassie a questioning look.

"Baal once gave himself up to some very bad men to save me and Seth from harm. I'd trust him in a heartbeat," Cassie replied, and Ranata seemed satisfied.

"Okay, then."

CHAPTER THREE

RANATA QUICKLY AGREED to Baal's demands because it would get her out of this place, but also, her gut told her to trust the woman named Cassie. As soon as the opportunity presented itself, however, she'd head out on her own. The sooner the better for her.

"I need a photo of your sister and any information you can give me on where she was last. Where she likes to hang out. You know the drill, I'm sure."

She kept pace beside him as they climbed a set of steps. "I have a photo of her back at my place."

"Perfect. I'll take you there, and you can grab whatever you'll need to be comfortable." He stopped and touched her arm. "Oh, and Ranata, don't think about running off. You made a promise, and I take those seriously. Crossing me wouldn't be wise."

She stared at him and tried not to focus on his devastating good looks. He certainly didn't appear to be a dangerous man. No, he looked more like one who knew how to pleasure a woman. Lord knew his clothes hugged every inch of his body and gave a good indication of what lurked underneath.

"Are you threatening me?" She tipped her head back slightly to look at him.

The corner of his mouth lifted. "No, sugar, I don't threaten women. However, I do keep my promises, and I promise if you place yourself in danger again, you'll feel my wrath across that beautiful ass of yours." He extended his hand and waited for her to take it. "Shall we?"

Heat rose across her cheeks, and she hesitated for a moment before slipping her hand into his and wondered what his wrath would feel like. The fire from his touch kissed her skin and warmed her entire body. She'd been wrong about him. He was most definitely a dangerous man. Not the type who would endanger your life. No, he was more the kind who would steal your will and have you surrendering to him heart, body and soul. She'd need to take care while in his company or risk losing herself.

Before she came back to her senses, they were surrounded by blackness dotted with white lights. The next thing she knew, they stood in her living room.

"What the hell?" She dropped his hand.

"You were too out of it to remember our mode of travel the last time, but it beats the hell out of those long lines at the airport," he chuckled. "Oh, you okay? You look a bit green."

She did feel a little shaky and chalked it up to a really shitty day. "I'll be fine. Let me grab some things." Before he responded, she was in her bedroom and pulling down a small, worn-leather case. It was the only piece of luggage she owned and had once belonged to her grandmother. Placing it on the bed, she went and dug out a couple pairs of jeans, some tees and underwear then tossed them in the bag. She didn't need much since she wasn't planning to stick around.

Next, she went into the closet and found her old winter coat. She'd hidden a couple hundred dollars in the pocket. It would be enough to get her back home as soon as she got away from Baal. *How does he think to keep an eye on me if he's out searching for Raven?* She stuffed the wad of cash in her pants pocket and did a quick glance around the room. There was nothing else she needed in here.

The photo of Raven sat on a shelf in the living room, so she headed back that way and discovered the demon seated on the couch, arm thrown over the back and tapping his fingers. She hated to admit just looking at him sent butterflies swirling in her stomach. Any man that hot had to have issues. Then again, she'd been coherent enough to notice the other so-called immortals she'd met were nothing to sneeze at. *Good lord, Ranata, get a grip.* She needed to remind herself that although he had rescued her, and now offered to look for her sister, he still wasn't to be fully trusted. She wasn't sure she'd ever trust a man again. She hadn't been surprised about Clive, but Father Ryan had broken the last of her faith.

She walked to the shelf and grabbed the photo. A picture of her and Raven from the previous summer when they'd been swimming at the lake. It was one of the last times her family had been together and happy. Shortly after, their father had died, and Raven had started acting weird. When six months later their mother also passed, Raven became withdrawn. Ranata would give anything to have her sister back.

She forced tears down and handed the photo to Baal. "This is Raven."

BAAL TOOK the framed picture from Ranata's hands and studied it. The two girls appeared much alike. Both wore their black hair long, but where Raven had brown eyes, Ranata had eyes that rivaled any tropical lagoon. Their blue depths had him wanting to see how much they darkened when she was in the throes of passion, and he most definitely wanted to be the one responsible.

"What can you tell me about her? Where did you last see her?"

Ranata plopped in a chair. "I think she was into the occult."

He schooled his features. The likelihood of finding Raven alive would be next to none, especially with Lowan lurking in the human realm and all the idiots trying to appease the devil by offering human sacrifices. "Tell me. Was she a virgin?"

She chewed her lip. "As far as I know, yes. I know it seems strange in this day and age, but she wanted to wait." She cocked her head. "Why?"

He went to the ottoman in front of her chair and sat down. "I'm not going to lie, and I refuse to sugarcoat anything."

The rise and fall of her chest increased and he tried not to notice her breasts under the tight tee she wore. "I appreciate that. Tell me what you know."

"Lowan is an evil demigod whose father was a demon overlord and mother a guardian. Try mixing a demon and vampire, sprinkle in a grandfather who's a god, and you have one fucking mess. He's been locked in Hell for centuries, and now, he's managed to find his way here."

That plump pink lip of hers found its way between her teeth, and he had to stifle a groan.

"I know I should be in shock right now, but for some reason, I'm not. Continue."

"Good girl. I need you to stay calm and focused. Anyway, the demon activity you see is because of him, and if your sister was involved in occult activity and a virgin, she is in serious trouble." He pulled in a deep breath. He'd promised not to lie. "She may already be dead."

Tears filled her eyes but remained unshed. "She can't be gone. Raven's all I've got left in this crummy world."

He wanted to know more, but his senses didn't care for the stench filling his nose. "We've gotta go. Now." He grabbed Ranata by the arms and jerked her to him. He didn't wait for a reaction from her. Instead, he flashed them from the small room and into his penthouse. She pushed away and glared at him.

"What the hell?"

He didn't respond but walked to the phone and picked it up. "I need you up here." In seconds, Jax flashed into the room, and Ranata screeched.

"You didn't tell me you had company," Jax said.

He shrugged. *She knows what I am.* He turned to face her. "Ranata, this is Jax. He's a powerful Draki—or in words you'll understand, a dragon."

She blinked. "A what?"

He ignored her and faced Jax. "There were demons surrounding her home. I'm going back to find out why. Don't let her out of your sight." He stormed across the room and punched his code into the keypad on the wall. The lock clicked, and he swung open the door to reveal a room full of weapons.

"Wait! Oh, my lord!" Ranata stepped in behind him. "Will you look at all this?"

He gave a short laugh. "I am looking, sugar." He pulled his favorite vest off the mannequin. It was already weighed down with daggers of various sizes, and he slipped it on. Next, he grabbed a pair of double-edged blades. They made slicing the head off most any demon a piece of cake. He turned to leave and found Ranata with her arms crossed and a lethal glare pinned on him.

"You can't just bring me here, announce something about demons surrounding my home and leave a dragon for a bodyguard without further explanation."

He moved past her. "I can, and I am." He didn't wait for a response. Instead, he flashed and left Jax to deal with his fallout.

RANATA WAS MOMENTARILY STUNNED, but quickly shook it off and replaced it with anger. She marched past the man named Jax, who stood with a wide stance and crossed arms. He'd never even acknowledged her. She grabbed her bag and headed for what she prayed was the exit. When she reached for the handle and opened the door, an arm shot over her head and pushed it shut.

She wasn't sure if she should be frightened or irate. She'd go with irate, and she spun to face her captor.

"Listen. You don't need to involve yourself in this matter. Let me walk out, and we can forget this entire incident."

Tall, dark, and deadly handsome, he glared down at her. His eyes shifted from hazel to green then back so quickly she thought she'd imagined it. "You humans are all the same." His thick brows pinched down over those ever-changing eyes as he tried to stare her down.

"And what exactly does that mean?"

"It means you never listen. Don't you think the demon had a valid reason to tell you to stay put?"

"I think the demon—as you call him—needs to learn better communication skills. It certainly would go a long way." She turned and tried to open the door again, but it slammed shut.

"You can either step away and go sit on whatever piece of furniture you deem comfortable. Or, I can forcibly remove you. Your choice." His voice remained calm yet carried an edge leaving her to suspect he wouldn't hesitate to carry out his threat.

Ranata pulled in a slow breath and counted to ten before she turned around again. "You like to bully women?"

"And you like to throw accusations when you know nothing about me or my species? The demon wants you protected, and that is that."

Her cheeks heated with embarrassment. It was true. She had no idea who or what he was, and he was following orders. "Fine. I'll take up my issues with Baal when he returns." She moved around the man and walked back across the room, tossing her bag and taking a seat in a large, leather chair. "So, why don't you enlighten me about your species? Or are your communication skills as bad as the demon's?" She didn't know why she had to get in that last dig. The man actually tipped back his head and laughed which helped to lighten her mood. Slightly.

"It's as he told you. I'm a Draki, a dragon shifter." He'd moved to a matching chair across from her, and his eyes twinkled with amusement. "You don't look too surprised."

"After what I've seen in the past couple days, I'm feeling a bit shell-shocked. I mean demons, angels with fangs, why not men who can shift into dragons? It's all perfectly logical." At some point, she was bound to wake up and find this was all just one hellish nightmare. "So how do you fit into this amusement-park ride?"

He shrugged. "My leader told me to come here and help in any way I can, so here I am. You?"

She tried to hold back her tears. She'd not been kidding when she referred to this as an amusement-park ride. One minute, she was perfectly fine and logical. The next, she'd dipped into the abyss of depression and worry for her sister. "My sister has gone missing, and somehow, I almost ended up a sacrifice to a demon. Just your average day." Again, she threw in an edge of humor. It was either find a way to cope or break. She refused to break.

"I see. Sorry about your sister. I hope she's okay."

She stared at her feet for what seemed an eternity. "All this drama must be normal everyday stuff for you. I had no idea any of this existed."

"Just run of the mill for me. Unfortunately, it's a rude awakening for your kind, and many will die."

"Can you be any colder about it?" There had been no undertones of remorse. His statement had been matter-of-fact.

He leaned forward, his elbows on his knees. "I am a warrior, and I have seen many die. I've even been the cause of some of those deaths."

She shivered. "I'll try not to think about that."

"You have nothing to fear from me. Matter of fact, you should feel safe under Baal's protection. He's a powerful demon, and one many will not mess with."

An idea struck her. "What can you tell me about him?"

"Other than he has a sister who's mated to my leader, and he's well liked among all the immortals? Nothing."

Well, so much for gaining any useful information.

CHAPTER FOUR

BAAL FLASHED to the top of a hill that conveniently overlooked Ranata's small home. He counted four demons and... *No fucking way!* He wasted no time in flashing behind the man and sticking the point of his dagger into his back.

"Tell me, Chaval, why do you care about one little human?"

The warrior cocked his head so he could look over his shoulder at Baal. "I could ask you the same, but do you really think you can take me?"

Baal knew his chances of winning any fight with Chaval were slim to a big fat zero. The man was a Sumari, half-demon and half-fae. A lethal combination who now worked for Lowan for some reason.

"What made you switch sides?" Baal kept a wary eye on the demons who surrounded them but stayed confident they would keep their distance as long as he held the upper hand and a blade to their leader's back.

"You, more than anyone, know things are not always as they appear. I can only tell you this." He lowered his voice. "Raven is now

Lowan's mistress, and for the present, she's safe. As for Ranata? She is more than either you or she realizes. Her past is key to her secret, and you must protect her at all costs."

Baal pressed the blade deeper. "What the fuck does that mean?"

Chaval broke free and faced Baal. In the blink of an eye, he shot out a burst of power and decapitated the other demons, dropping them to the ground. Baal dared not send out his own magic to fight him. Fae drew their power from others, and he wouldn't feed Chaval anymore.

"You kill your flunkies?" Baal inquired.

Chaval waved his hand, turned the bodies to ash and sent them scattering in the breeze. "They were casualties of a most unfortunate battle and the only way I could allow you to walk out of here alive without anyone's knowledge."

Something was off with this entire conversation. At one time, Chaval had been one of the good guys, but he'd been seen fighting side by side with Lowan during their last battle. "What's really going on with you?"

Chaval faded. "I'm not what I currently appear to be. Just remember, protect the girl with your life. If you don't, I will kill you personally."

He vanished, and Baal was left scratching his head. "Son of a bitch." He needed to see his sister. She was the only one he could confide in, and hopefully, before he did something stupid. Seconds later, he stood in the center of Lileta's kitchen.

"Your mate out of the castle?" He kissed her on the cheek.

"Yes. Off fighting, which is where I figured you'd be." She pulled him into a hug. "I've missed you." Then she pushed him to arm's length. "What's wrong?" They'd always been close and could read each other well.

He pulled up a seat at the table. "The gods can't seem to keep from fucking with our lives."

She settled in across from him. "What happened?" A look of concern caused creases around her beautiful golden eyes.

"You hear about the human Marcus and I rescued?"

She nodded.

"She belongs to me," he growled.

Her mouth dropped open. "I won't even ask whether you're sure because I know you are, but when did you figure it out?"

When had he become certain the raven-haired beauty was his mate? "Shortly after I found her at the guardian's compound and promised to find her missing sister." He ran his fingers through his hair. "Fuck me! I can't do this again."

She reached across the table and placed her hand on his. "I know. What are your plans?"

What are my plans? "Shit, I'm not sure. I'll keep my word to look for her sister. Right now, she's back in my penthouse with Jax watching over her."

"You know I'll do whatever I can to help you." She squeezed his hand. "I'm sure you realize how difficult it will be to keep from claiming her."

He leapt from his chair and knocked it over in the process. "I need to stay away from her. It's the only way."

Lileta shook her head. "Have you considered talking to Marcus? He would understand your situation."

He fisted his hands. "You're the only one who knows my past, and I have no desire to rehash it."

"You know I love you, but I think you're approaching this all wrong. You're going to end up hurt in the end."

He leaned over the table. "That's where you're wrong. I don't intend to give my heart to any woman ever again. Unlike Marcus, who could transform his mate into a vampire, I'm unable to make Ranata a demon." He straightened. "I have something to take care of."

He moved around the table and kissed her on the cheek then flashed from her home. He probably should have mentioned his encounter with Chaval, but he wasn't even sure how to explain it. The thought of telling Ranata her sister was with Lowan caused his gut to roll, but not near as much as the idea Ranata belonged to him.

RANATA CROSSED her legs and jiggled her foot. She had more nervous energy than she knew what to do with and needed a good run. "This place got a gym?" She eyed Jax.

"The hotel has one, of course, but Baal has a private one I'm sure he'd let you use."

At the mention of the demon, he appeared in front of them. Ranata stopped jiggling her foot and jumped from her chair. "Well?"

He looked at her then quickly diverted his gaze to Jax as he walked across the room to the kitchen where he opened the fridge and grabbed a container of orange juice. He poured a large glass and downed half of it. Before she could say a word, he was in front of her and in her face.

"Who or what are you exactly?" His tone indicated he was less than pleased.

"I don't understand. What happened while you were gone?"

"You want me to leave?" Jax interjected.

"No. Stay." Baal's eyes never left her, and she had to keep from fidgeting under his stare. "Maybe, you can sense what she is. I only pick up human."

Ranata took a step back and looked between the two men. "You want to tell me what you're talking about?"

"I sense nothing, but you know my dragon has a better nose than I do," Jax replied.

Baal turned his head. "Don't you fucking dare. Last time you shifted in here, I had to remodel."

"Okay, seriously. Do you have a lead on my sister or not?" She rubbed her arms, trying to relieve some anxiety. It didn't work.

"I was told she's Lowan's mistress and doing well," Baal snarled.

"W-what? Isn't that the demon or demigod you told me about

earlier?" She continued to rub her arms and paced. "I-I need to get her out of there." She stopped and looked at him, her eyes pleading. "Do you know where she is?"

"Do you have a death wish? And no, I don't."

Her brows pinched down at Baal's question. "Of course, I don't, but she's my sister!"

He huffed. "I realize that, but what exactly do you think you're going to do? Waltz in, grab her and waltz out?" Baal asked.

"I don't know! I thought you were the expert here." Tears threatened to spill again.

"Seriously. You don't need me here to bear witness to your banter." Jax rose from his seat.

"You're right. They need help killing demons," Baal commanded.

Jax clapped his hands together and rubbed. "Now, we're talking." He gave a slight bow to Ranata. "While it was a pleasure to meet you, I'm a warrior, not a babysitter. Good luck with your sister." He vanished before she could reply, and she had a sudden urge to throw up again.

The demon focused on her once more. "Now that he's gone, maybe, you'll come clean and share what's going on."

She was tired as hell of his games and wanted to be done with it, so she headed for the door. This time, she was determined to make a hasty exit. Grabbing the handle, she half-expected Baal to come up behind her. Instead, the handle refused to turn, and her skin prickled. She whirled to face the demon who still stood across the room. Fury and panic sent her blood to the boiling point.

"Let me go!"

Wind whipped around her. A lamp on a side table fell to the floor. Glass shattered in the distance along with her nerves.

"Stop it! Why are you doing this?" She placed her arms over her head and ducked to avoid flying debris. A hard body rammed into her then pinned her to the floor. Baal's lips were next to her ear.

"But I'm not the one doing this, princess. You are."

BAAL COVERED Ranata's body to protect her from the furniture flying across the room. He didn't know how, but the conditions in his penthouse had gone from calm to an F2 tornado in a matter of seconds. Each time he tried to subdue it, things grew worse.

"Princess, you need to stop whatever it is you're doing before you rip up my entire home." Though he had to admit, he loved the feel of her soft curves beneath him. She fit him like a glove.

"But I'm not doing this. I can't do stuff like this."

Somehow, he had to get her to calm down. His magic only made it worse.

"Ranata." He cupped her face and forced her gaze to him. "Look at me. Think happy thoughts and try to calm down." Her body trembled beneath him. He'd fucked up royally and freaked her out, and now, she was trashing the place. No way in hell she was human. But what the fuck was she?

"Princess, focus on me, and we'll breathe together. Ready?"

She nodded.

"Okay. Slow, deep breath in. Hold it...and let it out." A chair whizzed past his head. "Happy thoughts and deep breath. Hold, one, two, three and release." The wind calmed slightly. "Repeat." He breathed with her, but things weren't moving along fast enough to suit him. "Princess, I'm sorry for being a dick. I didn't mean to upset you. Calm down, and we'll talk. We'll figure this out together."

Everything stopped and crashed to the floor, but at least, it was quiet. He rolled off her and lay on his back staring at the ceiling. He sent out his magic to clean up the mess, but as he righted the kitchen table, Ranata rolled onto her stomach and vomited.

"Oh, god, I'm so sorry," she cried.

He jumped to his feet and scooped her up. As he walked to the bedroom, he turned her mess to ash and swept it away. "Don't worry about it. All taken care of." He laid her on his king-size bed and wondered why he'd brought her to his room and not one of the guest rooms.

You know damn well why you brought her here. It's where you want her. In your bed!

"Stay put." He went into the bathroom, grabbed a washcloth and wet it with cool water then came back and placed it on her forehead.

She pulled it down over her eyes. "I'm so sorry. I was suddenly so ill and had no control."

"It's okay. Are you feeling any better?" He went for a bottle of water from the mini-fridge then came back and sat on the edge of the bed. "Here, drink this."

She peeked out from beneath the washcloth, her embarrassment evident. "Thanks." She struggled to push herself to sitting. When she'd finally managed, she grabbed the bottle and took a big sip. "What the hell happened out there? Why'd you do that?"

He searched her eyes and sensed she wasn't lying. She had no clue what had happened. "I didn't start that. Matter of fact, the more magic I tried to use to stop it, the worse it got. Sugar, it was all you. You created that storm."

She rubbed her eyes. "But I can't levitate objects or create wind." Then she cracked a smile. "Though I'll admit, I had an urge to throw something at you."

Again, he sensed she was telling the truth. "Something strange is going on here."

She tried to hide a yawn.

"You need some rest. Stay here, and get some sleep. I'll be in the other room and later, when you're rested, we have a lot to talk about."

"I am really tired all of a sudden." She lay back and rolled to her side, tucking her hands up under her chin. Baal got up and walked from the room before he did something stupid, like forget he wasn't about to give his heart to any female.

As he stormed back to the living room, his thoughts strayed briefly. *She can't be fully human with the power she exhibited earlier. Maybe, I can claim her.* He poured a shot of tequila and downed it.

"And I must be fucking crazy to consider it." Baal needed someone to track Chaval and figure out what the warrior was up to. He'd ask his sister to do it, but her mate, Caleb would have his head. Besides, Baal would never put his sister in harm's way. He poured another shot then opened his mind to see whether his call would be answered.

Lucan? If you can hear me, I have a job for you.

CHAPTER FIVE

LUCAN CALLED to the shadows and commanded they form a circle around the three demons who'd terrorized a young girl on the street. What she'd been doing out after dark was beyond him. Didn't these people understand what a curfew was? His leader, Aidyn, had gone to the Vatican and spoken with the head honcho. Luckily, the Catholic church was on board with offering any cooperation they could to rid the world of the demon stench that had filtered up from Hell.

Officials issued a curfew in the hope of getting people off the street before dark to keep them safe. Humans flocked to the local churches. It hadn't taken long for word to spread that the demons couldn't enter. He chuckled to himself. If they only knew the spawn of Hell didn't give two shits about churches and their religious relics. What kept them at bay was Lucan and his brethren. They'd drank the water from the Cave of Knowledge, thus making their blood sacred. They cut themselves and traced blood crosses on the building so demons couldn't enter. Knowing people would seek refuge in their local churches, the guardians had protected those buildings first.

Now, it was time for the guardians to expose themselves. Aidyn would hold a public broadcast in a few days that would hopefully accomplish that. Lucan still believed it was a bad idea. They should have just let Gabriel, and his armies of winged warriors play the role of good guys while Lucan and his brethren stayed hidden in the background and did what they were created to do.

Protect humanity.

Humans didn't need to know their protectors had fangs and drank blood. They were better off with their illusions of the winged angels.

Lucan produced his sword. "You fuckers picked the wrong street to play on." The shadows, still under his command, kept the evil corralled while he swung the blade taking off all three heads in one swipe.

Lucan? If you can hear me, I have a job for you.

He wiped the blood from his blade and wondered what the demon, Baal, would have need of him to do. Normally, Lucan liked to work alone. He was having a difficult time since Marcus and Seth had found their mates. Add to that the recent death of one of their brethren, Garin, and he felt like the odd man out. Things were changing, and Lucan hated change.

Not that he'd begrudge his friends' happiness. He was thrilled Marcus and Seth had both found their mates and thus reversed the curse Drayos had placed on them centuries earlier. Lucan lived with the curse every day. The darkness that resided inside every guardian slowly spread until it consumed them and snuffed out their light, making them blood-thirsty killers. However, Lucan didn't want to fight the darkness. He welcomed the extra power it brought him with open arms.

With a flick of his wrist, he commanded the shadows into a mini-funnel cloud that picked up the remains of the demons and swept them away. Then he locked onto Baal's location and flashed.

"What do you want, demon?" He stood in Baal's penthouse living room.

"You'll never guess who I had a strange encounter with?" Baal held up his hand. "I'll tell you. Chaval. I'd like you to figure out what he's been up to."

Lucan bared his fangs. "I'll tell you what he's been up to. He's a fucking traitor, and I thought you knew that."

"I sense otherwise. He didn't say anything to indicate what's going on, but he said things are not what they appear. He opened himself to me. The man's afraid. You and I both know Chaval fears nothing." Baal went on to explain his encounter with the Sumari warrior, and the more Lucan heard, the more intrigued he became. Chaval had been a childhood friend. What had made him side with their enemies? More important, what the hell was he afraid of?

"I trust your senses and agree, there's more here than we can see. I will search his homeland," Lucan replied.

Baal raised a brow. "Can you get in?"

"I can go anywhere. You forget, I control the shadow walkers. However, I'm curious why you don't ask your sister to do this?" Everyone knew her dark power was as strong as Lucan's.

"I don't want her involved. You in or not?"

Lucan didn't need to think about it. "I love a challenge. I'll go there now."

RANATA HAD no idea how long she'd been asleep, but her stomach rumbled in hunger. She threw her legs over the side of the bed, stood and padded out of the room. After a quick search, she found Baal in the kitchen, standing at the counter chopping some vegetables. A delicious aroma wafted from behind him.

He looked up and smiled. "Hope you're hungry and you like pasta."

Her stomach growled in response. "I'm starved. What is that? God, it smells delicious." Her mouth watered.

He placed the vegetables into a wooden bowl then gave them a light toss. "It's an old family recipe."

She stepped to the stove and looked into the large simmering pot. A thick red sauce bubbled, and the smell that followed the steam upward caused her stomach to knot in hunger. "Mmm, how long before we can eat?"

"Go sit. You can start with a salad, and the rest will follow."

Ranata complied and took a seat at the black lacquer table where two place settings had been laid out. "I didn't know demons could cook."

Baal placed a plate full of greens, tomatoes, cucumbers, various colored peppers and olives in front of her. "The dressing is also an old family recipe, and yes, we cook."

She picked up her fork while he poured her a glass of red wine. "I guess I just assumed since you live in a penthouse and own a casino..."

"What? That I'd have people waiting on me hand and foot?" He shook his head. "Not really my style. Don't get me wrong, I like fine things, but at heart, I'm a warrior. I like getting dirty." He pulled out the chair across from her and sat. For some reason, a picture of him covered with dirt and wearing a ripped shirt popped into her head.

Dear god. She diverted her attention to her salad and dove in. "This is really good."

"Thanks. So, I thought we should discuss what happened earlier today," he said between bites.

"I told you. I'm unable to make objects float around the room." The remembrance of earlier caused her to shiver. It had scared the shit out of her.

"I know, and I can sense you're telling the truth."

She looked up. "Really? You can tell when people are lying?"

"I can sense all emotions. Demons usually prey on people when they're most vulnerable. However, some of us have evolved beyond the need to torture."

"Oh. Well, that's a good thing then." Though she didn't know him, she couldn't picture him torturing someone.

"When I went to your home, it was surrounded by demons. Their leader and I had an interesting chat about you and your sister," Baal continued.

Fear gripped her gut and twisted. She recalled their earlier conversation. "You said she's with Lowan. How do we get her back?"

Baal set his fork on the table. "Let me give you a *Lowan* lesson. He is a demigod. That means he has more power in his pinkie than an entire army of demons." His forehead creased. "He's the fucking reaper on steroids."

She fought to control her emotions. Tears wouldn't get Raven out of trouble. "So, you're saying there's no way to reach her?"

He shook his head. "I never say never. I just don't know the *how* yet. Maybe, you have the answer."

"Me?"

"I said my discussion included you. I was told to protect you at all costs. Something about your past is the key to your secret. You are more than you realize. So...what's your secret, Ranata?"

"I-I don't know what that means." She pushed aside her empty salad plate and watched him rise and clean up their dirty dishes, carrying them to the kitchen. Moments later, he returned and placed a steaming plate of spaghetti in front of her. She dove in, wanting to know whether it tasted as good as it smelled. It was better.

They were halfway through their meal before he spoke again. "Listen up, sugar. It's time you spilled. What are you hiding that I should know about?"

She'd be damned if she'd rehash her past. It wasn't anyone's business. *Besides, it has nothing to do with finding Raven.* "I'm not hiding anything. Your friend is delusional."

He studied her. His golden gaze penetrated into her soul until she shifted in her seat.

"Did you forget, sweetheart, I can detect when you're lying? Care to try again?" He reached for his glass of wine and took a sip. "Who are your parents?"

"Robert and Stella Aldrich. Know them?" She laced her reply with sarcasm.

"No. Who were your real parents?" He pushed aside his plate and leaned back in his chair.

She picked up her napkin, wiped her mouth then tossed it on the table. "They were my real parents, and this conversation is done." She stood and took two steps when she ran into him. "How the hell?"

"I'm faster than you, and there are a few other things you should know." He stood so close she felt his hot breath across her lips.

"What's that?" she whispered.

"My favorite pastimes are fucking and fighting. I excel at both."

Why the hell did that statement turn her on? "I need to know this why?"

"The reason I excel is because I spend a lot of time practicing, and the reason I practice is so I'm not tempted by my demonic urges. I told you, some of us have evolved beyond the need to torture." He cupped her chin. "I don't hurt innocents, but that doesn't mean I can't take what I want from you." His gaze burned darker. "The craving to prey on human weakness is with me every day."

The lump in her throat rose higher. "How can you say you don't hurt people then?"

"Oh, sugar, there will be no pain. On the contrary. The pleasure you'll feel will have you begging to tell me anything I want to know." He released her. "But I don't want to play dirty, so let's say we sit down and start over."

She only needed a moment to contemplate her next move, and logic demanded she comply. Ranata managed her way across the living room on wobbly legs and curled up in a chair. Baal came over and refilled her a glass of wine.

"This might help you relax."

Relaxation was exactly what she needed, so she accepted the glass and took a big sip. "So, what exactly am I supposed to tell you?" she asked as he settled on the couch across from her and a fire lit on its own in the fireplace.

"Start with who were your real parents."

Figures he'd make her dive right into the most painful part of her past. She took another sip of wine. "I don't know who my real father is. My mother..." Visions of the beautiful woman with long black hair and brilliant blue eyes floated back to her. She shoved aside the pain.

"My mother dropped my sister and I off to the local nuns when I was five. She said she'd return later that night, but she never came back. I was too young to understand she'd dumped us at an orphanage. I only knew that I must have done something terribly wrong to make her abandon us." Tears stung her eyes, and her chest tightened. "But Raven was only a year old, and she didn't deserve that." Ranata had tried so hard to put that day behind her, and rehashing the past was like ripping open an old wound. It hurt like hell.

LUCAN SHIFTED into a black mist as he approached the portal that led to Chaval's home world. It was the only way he could enter since the magic woven around it was meant to keep intruders out. However, as mist he was able to squeeze through the tiny pinholes that always dotted any portal—even one created by the fae.

He pushed his way through and into the other side where darkness had fallen. His planning had been perfect, and he stayed in the form of mist so he could blend into the black night. As he zipped high above the ground, he was overcome with a sense of emptiness.

This is odd. Where the hell is everyone? The kingdom of Thyldan was home to at least a thousand fae.

Lucan hovered in front of the castle and reached out with his senses. Empty. He slipped through the keyhole and shifted to human form on the other side. In the great hall, large wooden tables and chairs were busted into kindling-sized pieces. Broken ceramic littered the floor. Evidence of a battle was everywhere. He took a deep breath, and the coppery scent of blood coated the back of his throat.

Had they all been slain?

"Impossible." Lucan made his way around the debris and headed up the stairs, knowing full well Chaval would never have let his people die. Or would he? Had the demon side of him gone completely insane and snapped?

He strode past several open doors, sticking his head through each to look inside. Most of them were guest quarters, and he remembered that the royal family held the entire upper floor, so he headed for the stairs on the other side and took two at a time.

When he reached the third level, he went directly to Chaval's suite. The door stood wide open so he walked through. On first glance, everything looked in order. The sitting room was in pristine condition with not a speck of dust anywhere, and nothing appeared out of place. He opened his senses and was again met with emptiness, so he moved to the other rooms in the apartment. All were empty and looked as if nothing had been touched in ages. If memory served him, Chaval's mother, sister, and aunt who was the fae queen had rooms on the same floor. He flashed back into the hall and went to the next apartment. This one belonged to Chaval's sister, and after a quick sweep, he was no more informed than he'd been when he'd arrived. He decided to go straight for the queen's chamber and flashed into the sitting room.

Blood stained the floor.

"Fuck. This isn't good." There was only one way to find out what the hell had happened here. He would have to summon the shadows and force them to divulge their secrets.

He closed his eyes and dove into the deep, dark recesses of his mind. The inky spot on his soul stirred in response as he called forth the shadows and took command of them. Whenever Lucan used his gift, Drayos's curse grew stronger within him. Lucan had already realized he'd likely die at the hands of one of his brethren because he'd never find his mate in time to save him. Even if he were lucky enough to locate her, would she accept him? Doubtful. The darkness had fucked him up and made it impossible for him to have any sexual relations unless the woman was bound and totally at his mercy. His mate would have to be as messed up as he was. Meanwhile, he'd continue to do his job and fight off the curse for as long as he could.

He'd avoid Marcus and his examinations. Lucan didn't need anyone telling him his clock was ticking.

The shadows swirled around him, whispering, tempting him to join them. He fought the urge to succumb. "Show me what happened to the one who lived here," he commanded.

In slow motion, they played out a bloody scene and revealed their secrets. Lucan stood motionless, unable to believe what he witnessed. "Son of a bitch!" Even he understood the consequences of what had happened. The mortal world was in deeper peril than any of them realized. If Lowan was able to reach the fae and overtake them, no one was safe.

CHAPTER SIX

BAAL STARED at the woman across from him. Her pain filled the room and burrowed itself deep into his soul. She belonged to him, and he knew he could ease it, but at what cost to his heart? The erection he sported demanded he take advantage of her, and it caused him to shift in his seat.

He leaned forward. "Ranata, look at me."

She brought her gaze to his.

"You don't have to hurt like this. I can take away your pain." It wasn't a lie. He could, and he wanted to, but in the end, would he choose to be honorable and use his power to do it or would he seduce her? One side of him warred with the other, and seduction was on the fast track to becoming the victor. "Do you remember her name? Your mother?"

"Iris."

He knew an Iris. She was a beautiful woman who had long black hair and blue eyes. *Not possible.* To his knowledge, she'd never had any daughters. "Do you remember anything else about your mother?"

Her pain filled the room again. Maybe, he should give her a break.

"Baal." Mist drifted into the room and swirled into the form of Lucan.

Ranata gasped and pushed back into her chair.

"Don't worry. Lucan is a rather gifted guardian. The only one among them who can shift." Baal stood and silently thanked the warrior for interrupting and keeping Baal from making a grave mistake with Ranata. "What did you discover?"

Lucan eyed Ranata.

"Don't worry. Whatever you have to say can be said in front of her."

The dark warrior strode to the bar and poured whiskey into a glass then chugged it down. "We have big, fuckin' problems. The place is deserted." He poured another. "I had to summon the shadows to divulge their secrets." He tipped back the glass and emptied it. "The queen is dead."

Baal slid in next to Lucan. "Son of a bitch. Pour me one."

Ranata jumped up and approached with caution. "The queen?"

He faced her. "Yes. Iris was the fae queen and—" Realization smacked him in the head. His mind did a quick review of the earlier conversation with Chaval, and now, everything started to make sense. He was willing to stake his life on Ranata being the daughter of the fae queen.

"Fuck it." He grabbed the bottle and took a long swig then wiped his mouth. "Your mother was the fae queen."

The sight of Lucan and Ranata staring at him with their mouths agape would have been hysterical had he been a simple observer. Except he was way more than that. Fate had handed him the daughter of a dead queen to protect. Wasn't that the fucking cherry on the cream. He shoved his fingers through his hair.

"Fuck me running," Baal growled.

Lucan arched a brow. "This story should be good and worthy of another bottle." He reached into the cabinet where Baal kept the spares and pulled out a full bottle of Jack then headed to the couch where he pulled off the cap and tossed it into the fire. "Start talkin', demon."

Baal fisted his bottle and headed for a chair. "Ranata, this is a story that calls for drinking. Refill your glass, you're gonna need it." She hesitated for only a moment before pouring more wine and making herself comfortable on the other end of the couch from Lucan.

"Iris would have been Chaval's aunt. She was a powerful fae queen who worked tirelessly to bring her people back into favor with the rest of immortal society. Her younger sister, Chaval's mother, slept with a demon and caused a big rift between the two species. The fae are rather particular when it comes to tainting their bloodline and were not fond of a demon in their midst."

He took a swig.

"Matter of fact, that door swings both ways. Most immortals aren't fond of the fae since a few bad apples were caught stealing magic from others." Lucan scowled. "We get a little pissy when that happens, and we get nervous every time a Sumari is born. They have demon strength and the dark fae's ability to absorb any magic around them and use it at will."

Baal nodded in agreement. "Sexual unions between a demon and fae always bear a male child, and always a Sumari. It's a matter of which side the child takes after most and with which parent they are raised that determines how they turn out. In Chaval's case, he spent most of his childhood with his father, raised as a demon. Later, he went to stay with his mother and refused to take any shit from the fae. They didn't dare mess with him so he was accepted into their society. I'm pretty sure Iris hoped he would become sort of an ambassador between the two species."

Ranata looked at Lucan then back to Baal, confusion clouding her features.

"The fae have little magic," Baal said. "A few spells and such, but their best defense is that they can use any magic around them against their enemy. That's what fuels their power and probably the only reason they allowed Chaval into their society. On rare occasions, a Sumari will have the ability to make their own magic. When that happens, it's like being on steroids. Their power can keep feeding upon itself, and if they lose control, it's equivalent to a nuclear bomb." Another long swig. "Devastating doesn't even begin to describe it."

"I feel so lost here," Ranata finally said.

"From what I could gather, Lowan was responsible for the queen's death. Most of the people fled, but Chaval's sister was taken." Lucan leaned forward and pinned a dark gaze on Baal. "I don't doubt that's how Lowan gained control over Chaval. Otherwise, demigod or not, Lowan would have never gained the upper hand."

"Did you see Lowan actually kill the queen?" Baal asked.

"No, the murderer was cloaked, but Lowan had a hand in it, whether directly or not," Lucan replied.

"Wait, but how do I fit into this? What makes you think the queen was my mother?"

"Because you look like her, and it makes sense. Iris was a smart woman, and she must have known danger was forthcoming and hid you. Otherwise, she wouldn't have left her daughters. Had she not been killed, she would have come back for you. What puzzles me is why. She had a mate who was fae, so what caused her to sleep with a human?"

Panic set in. Even if he'd considered it, there was no way he could mate with Ranata. She was fae, and he refused to bring more Sumari into the world. There hadn't been many over the past several years, but the few who had been allowed to survive—Chaval being one of them—had control over their powers. The others had been sentenced to death at a young age because they were a danger to themselves and everyone around them. Baal couldn't chance having to destroy his own son. It would devastate him.

SHE HAD to be going insane. Ranata had no explanation for all the craziness that seemed to surround her. Demons had taken over. Her sister was a mistress to a demigod, and her mother had been a fae queen? It was too unreal for words. She shook her head.

"No. It's all a coincidence. My mother simply had the same name as this fae, and maybe, they looked similar, but that's all."

"Really? Then explain to me how earlier you levitated everything in this room and threw it at my head?" Baal inquired.

Lucan laughed. "What the fuck did you do to piss her off, demon?"

Baal jumped up and stormed to the fireplace. The flames grew taller and more violent. "You took my power, Ranata, and used it against me. Whether you realized it or not." He spun to face them both. "The gods have finally lost it by choosing you as my mate."

"What the hell?" Lucan whispered. "She belongs to you?"

"Funny, isn't it? You know as well as I do that a fated mating between a demon and fae is rare. It's more likely for the two species to have a one-night stand then be on their way."

She grabbed her glass of wine and chugged it down. Was it possible she wasn't human? "I'm thirty years old. Why didn't I know I'm different before this? And wait... What do you mean by choosing me as your mate?" She stood, her anger flaring. "If you think I'm sleeping with you, you're fucking nuts!"

The demon slipped in front of her before she had even realized it. *Damn, he's fast.*

"Just so we're clear, I have no intention of sleeping with you. Matter of fact..." The front door swung open. "You're free to go. I have no desire to sleep with one eye open, and I certainly don't want you using my power against me again. It's obvious you're unstable, and I can't take any chances." He shoved a wad of cash at her. "Take this. No strings. Just consider it payment for your inconvenience."

She fisted her hands to keep from slugging him then took the money. "Fine. I never asked to come here in the first place, and you've done nothing but go back on your word at every turn." Wasting no time, she shoved the cash into her jeans pocket and stormed out the door. Spotting an elevator at the end of the hall, she marched over and pushed the button. She refused to look behind her because if Baal was watching, she might figure out a way to torch his ass. Instead, she stepped into the elevator and faced the back wall until the doors closed. When she turned, the light indicated there were thirty-nine floors before she'd reach the lobby. There was time to kill. Reaching into her pocket, she pulled out the wad of cash and counted.

"Holy shit!"

She went through it again. There was two thousand dollars in one-hundred-dollar bills. She was half tempted to turn around and go back. This was way too much money, but she recognized she was in another state with the small amount of cash she'd grabbed from home. She'd left without her bag and had only the clothes on her back. She'd consider this a loan and figure out a way to pay him back. Someday.

When the elevator finally stopped and the doors opened, a man dressed in a black suit greeted her.

"Miss Aldrich, I've been instructed by Mr. Danger to take you wherever you request. The limo is at your disposal. Should you desire to fly back home, I can have the private jet ready by the time we reach the airport."

"Mr. Danger, huh?" The name seemed fitting, but she had to wonder if he had chosen it for a reason. Two things were certain, Ranata hadn't expected the cash, and she'd certainly hadn't anticipated a limo or a jet. He must really want her out of town. She gathered her wits. "Yes. I need to go back to South Dakota." She had no idea why she was going back home and wasn't even sure it was safe. Baal had mentioned finding demons there, and now, she worried if they'd still be hanging around. However, she had nowhere else to go, and all her belongings were there. She needed somewhere familiar to think and plan a way to find her sister.

The man escorted her from the elevator and down a corridor. Outside, darkness had fallen, and she realized she had no idea what time of day it was. "Excuse me?"

"Yes, ma'am?"

"Can you tell me the time?"

"It's one-thirty a.m." He opened the limo door, and she scooted inside. "The driver has instructions to take you to the airport where the plane will be waiting. Is there anything else, Miss Aldrich?"

"No. Thank you for your kindness."

He tipped his head. "Have a safe flight." The door closed, and the limo pulled into traffic.

Ranata hardly noticed the bright lights of the strip through the tears that filled her eyes. Never had she felt more alone or confused in her life. Baal had promised to help find her sister. He'd even seemed concerned with her welfare, but something had changed. Could she really be responsible for the craziness that had happened earlier in his suite? Was it possible her real mother had been a fae queen? So many questions and no one to turn to for answers. Going it on her own had always been her lot in life, and this would prove no different. She'd suck it up like always and search for Raven. If she were capable of magic, she'd figure that out, too. She didn't need help from anyone, and most certainly not that damn demon.

"I CAN'T BELIEVE you just let her go." Lucan watched Baal wear a path in the carpet.

Baal stopped his pacing long enough to swig from his bottle and throw the guardian a death glare. "You know a powerful fae can destroy a demon."

"That's not the real reason. I don't sense enough power in her to do you in," Lucan stated.

He was right. It was fear. Bone-chilling fear sank its ugly claws into him. "Fuck. I can't risk my son being one of the unlucky ones who must be destroyed. No way in hell can I face that." He slammed his bottle on the table. Burning anger replaced his fear. "I need to go pick a fight with the god, Zarek. Can you sniff around and see about Chaval's sister? Maybe find the ones involved in the queen's murder. Something tells me it was an inside job."

The guardian shook his head. "Zarek will zap your ass if you piss him off, and yeah, I'll snoop." He rubbed his hands together. "Something tells me the trail will lead me straight into Hell."

"I'm sure you'll enjoy the trip, and if I'm still alive later, you can regale me with the stories." He didn't wait for a reply but flashed from the room and straight to the Temple of the Gods. Unlike his guardian friends, he didn't need special permission to enter their realm.

He climbed the steps to Zarek's temple two at a time. The king of gods had better be home, or Baal would simply have to entertain himself, and when he got bored things never turned out well. The front door opened on its own as soon as he approached, and the minute Baal crossed the threshold, Zarek stood on the other side. The god wore only jeans and a glare.

"I'll warn you now, behave or feel my wrath," Zarek stated.

"Fuck you, asshole." Baal stepped right into the god's space and pinned him with his own stare. Zarek stood only a few inches taller, so Baal casted his glance upward. "Why?"

Zarek crossed his arms and took a step backward. "You really do have a death wish."

"I might as well. I mean...you're the one who decided my mate should be a fae. A fucking fae! Are you nuts?" He felt the vein in his temple twitch. He'd be lucky if his head didn't explode.

"First off, when you decide to storm into my home, you will fucking kneel," Zarek growled and used his power to force Baal to his knees without so much as batting an eyelash. "Secondly, your mate was not my choice. Hades decided your fate. You should be thankful I was kind enough to allow him to grant you one at all."

"Then I shall deal with Hades on this matter," Baal snarled.

"With pleasure." Zarek flicked his wrist, and Baal tumbled into a black hole. Moments later, he landed on his ass directly at the foot of Hades' throne.

"Well, what took you so long, my demon?" the god laughed.

CHAPTER SEVEN

HAD CIRCUMSTANCES BEEN DIFFERENT, Ranata would have enjoyed flying on a private jet. As it was, it only gave her time to think about her predicament. Saying she was screwed was an understatement, and after a taxi ride home, she'd planted herself in front of the TV to watch the world news. Things had gone from crazy to insane. Human fatalities were in the thousands, and officials weren't even sure how accurate their numbers were. There was simply no way to tell.

She watched reruns of a press conference with the guardian named Aidyn and a winged man who called himself Gabriel. The media had gone wild with their questions, but the two men had remained calm and answered everything asked of them. They didn't seem to pull any punches either. When asked how many more lives would be lost, Aidyn hadn't given false hope. "I wish I knew, but this war will not end overnight." The press room had grown silent as his words had sunk in and the realization of what they dealt with hit home. The evilest of beings had come to sink his claws into their world, and he wasn't about to let go. If humanity wanted to survive, they'd have to fight or submit to his will.

Still riveted to the TV, Ranata soon learned Raven's possible location. The guardian, Aidyn, said Lowan had taken up residence at the White House. If he were really there, so was her sister.

Ranata jumped to her feet and ran to get her laptop in her bedroom then settled on her bed. She popped it open and did a Google search on fae. It seemed silly, and she wasn't even sure she'd find anything, but it was worth a shot. She clicked on the website for the Urban Dictionary and read:

A FAE IS A HUMANOID, *mystical creature that wields great power in magic and elements, usually have antennae and insect-like wings and are short. Faes are otherwise known as fairies and are commonly used in RPs.*

SHE JUMPED up and ran to the mirror over her dresser and lifted her shirt. "I'd better not get wings." She did a slow turn and craned her neck to look at her back.

"Don't believe what you read on the internet. We don't have wings," a deep voice came from the doorway and caused her to jump, yanking her shirt back down. When she turned toward it, she gasped.

"Who the hell are you?" She stared at a man who was a good foot taller than her. Pointed ears poked out from straight, white hair that fell to his wide shoulders. Two horns curled from the top of his head.

She took a step back, and his blue eyes followed her.

"Don't be frightened of me, but where is Baal? I told him to protect you."

"I... You must be Chaval?" she stammered, remembering something about his species being unstable.

"Yes, and you're not safe here." He moved toward her, and she took another step back. "Where is the demon?"

"We didn't see eye-to-eye."

"Explain!"

She didn't take getting yelled at very well. "I think *you* have some explaining to do. If I'm to understand correctly, my sister is with your leader. Why? And what exactly am I, and why do I need a demon to protect me?" She took a step forward and crossed her arms, hoping to show she was stronger than she felt.

He tossed his head back and laughed. "You have your mother's fire. This is good." His forehead furrowed. "I don't have much time before Lowan will look for me, so you're going to get a crash course. You're now the rightful queen of the fae. Your destiny is to save our people from a certain death and convince them to enter this war." His features softened. "Also, to continue your mother's work. She'd made big strides in regaining respect for the fae."

"What?" she whispered. "I know nothing about being a queen or fae. This can't be happening." She pinched herself. "Ouch! Shit, I was hoping to wake up."

Chaval moved closer and placed his hands on her shoulders. "Look. I know this all seems a bit much, but I've been keeping an eye on you since you were a child. You're a strong, determined woman, just like your mother. We need you. Trust fate to lead you down the right path." Lines formed around his eyes. "Don't let your mother's death be in vain. Come home, and let us teach you who you really are."

She took ragged breaths and swallowed her fear. It left a bitter taste in her mouth, but what could she say? The world outside had gone completely mad. "Will I be safe there?" She couldn't help Raven if she were dead.

"It will be the safest place for you."

She squared her shoulders. "Then I will do what's required of me."

BAAL JUMPED TO HIS FEET. "What the hell made you think selecting a fae as my mate was a good fucking idea?"

Hades stared at him. "Because she needs you."

"Since when does a fae need a demon, unless it's to steal our power?" Ranata had already tried to bring down destruction on his head. Granted, it turned out she had no idea what she was doing, but the fact remained she was a danger to him.

The demon god rose from his serpent-covered throne and towered over Baal. "Here's how this will play out. You will protect her at all costs. Ranata is only half-fae. Her father was a human, so she has little control over her powers."

Baal snorted. "I'll say."

Hades ignored the smart remark. "Choosing a demon ensures she will have a mate capable of protecting her, providing her with the power she'll need and teaching her how to control it. It will bring the demons and fae closer together, and hopefully, she'll be able to convince her people to enter the war. You two will become the ambassadors between the species." He lifted a small, beating heart from a silver tray offered by one of his minions and popped it into his mouth. "Your children will be beautiful."

Baal had always wanted children, but centuries earlier, he'd fallen in love with a human then lost his heart when she'd passed. He'd vowed to spend eternity alone. Plus, there was the Sumari thing hanging over his head. "Will they be Sumari since she is half-mortal?"

"No, not Sumari. You need not fear your children's death or hers. Her bond with you will ensure her immortality," Hades replied.

"You're assuming I'll agree to any of this."

The god's gaze narrowed, and red flashed in his eyes. "*You* assume you have a choice."

"Are you telling me I don't?" He fisted his palms and tried to push down his anger. He was getting sick and tired of higher ups running his life.

"I am telling you your fate has been decided. Whether you

choose to love your mate is up to you, but you *will* protect her and help her prepare for bringing her people back together."

Baal ground his teeth together. "What are you not telling me? I think you owe me the entire story since you've just fucked up my entire existence."

Hades shoved his hands behind his back, spun on the ball of his foot and took three steps away before stopping. He stood with his back to Baal, and defeat showed in his posture before he regained himself and spun back to Baal. "You're right. Iris came to me many years ago and begged for help. The fae had been experiencing a widespread, lethal virus that rendered them unable to use the power of any immortal. As you can imagine, this left them vulnerable to attack. The queen's best doctors searched for a cure with no luck. Finally, it was discovered that Lowan was responsible."

"He knew the fae would be the one adversary able to beat him."

Hades nodded. "Exactly, but how he managed we still don't know. Anyway, Iris had herself artificially inseminated by a human in the hope her children would be immune to the virus. Ranata is the oldest, and when she was born, they were confident she was immune, but Iris didn't want to leave anything to chance. Four years later, she was inseminated again and bore Raven. Both girls carry a potential cure within their blood, but the burden falls to Ranata."

"I still don't get how I fit into this fucked-up picture."

"Iris was already mated to one of her own when she bore both daughters. He was killed in a battle with an enemy shortly after Raven's birth. With the loss of her mate, she hid her daughters in the human realm to protect them. When the virus invaded her body, Lowan attacked and killed her." Hades walked back to his throne and sat. "I promised her, should anything happen, her eldest daughter would be mated to my best demon. Though your attitude is shit, I know I can count on you to protect her and help her save her race." He leveled his gaze. "It's time for you to let go of Beth and find some damn happiness."

Baal punched the stone wall and enjoyed the pain as the bones in his fist shattered and cut through his skin. He'd heal. His heart should have healed as well. He'd loved Beth with every fiber of his being, but he'd been responsible for her death. He'd broken her heart when he'd explained what he was and why he couldn't marry her. An immortal never knew when their fated mate would appear, and he feared the consequences if he stayed with Beth. They'd both been devastated, but she'd taken her life. He'd never forgiven himself.

"I let her die."

Hades sighed. "She chose her fate. Yes, you shouldn't have had a relationship with her, but for gods' sake that was forever ago. Move on, and make a choice to help your mate."

Baal studied the god. Something still didn't sit right with him. "I'm not buying your entire story. Why would a demon god grant a fae, even if she were a queen, such a favor?"

Hades clenched his jaw before closing his eyes and taking a deep breath. "I was once in love with Iris, but our fates were not to be intertwined." He opened his eyes. "She belonged to another, and I eventually moved on. When she came to me and begged for this favor, I could not say no."

"So, because you'd once had an affair, that made it okay to fuck with *my* fate?"

"No. It was because these events needed to be set in motion." Hades' fangs flashed. "Lowan must die. Now, come to me."

Baal knew he'd pressed his luck far enough, so he went before the demon god and knelt. Hades placed his palm atop Baal's head, and visions assaulted him. Thirty years of a young woman's life joined his own memories, and he knew Ranata better than she knew herself. She was a woman who had given of herself so others could have a better life. She was just like her mother, and now, he realized why she'd been chosen to rule. He'd mate with Ranata, and he would protect her, but his heart had to remain his own.

CHAVAL SMILED. "Smart woman. Let me tell you about your mother, my Aunt Iris." He gave Ranata a quick replay of her mother's life. How a virus had left the fae vulnerable and how Ranata and her sister had come to be born. As he told the story, she felt a sense of pride for her mother. The woman had sacrificed so much to save her people, and in the end, she'd lost her life.

She didn't forget about us.

"Your mother loved you both more than her life. She cried herself to sleep every night from the pain of missing you."

Knowing this made her heart heavy, and she wished she'd had the chance to know her mother and tell her mother how much she had been loved.

Ranata blinked back the tears. "Do you have a photo of my mother?"

"Not with me, but maybe there's one still back home." He moved to her and grasped her arms. "My sister is in Lowan's grip, so many of our people are either in hiding or dead. You must mate with the demon. I know the cure will be found in you, and we'll finally rebuild. Not to mention we are needed in this war."

The survival of an entire race sat on her shoulders, but if her mother could make so many sacrifices, so could she. She also wanted to know everything about the woman, and one way was to be around the people who knew her best.

"Well, he tossed me out, so I think you're out of luck on that one. Besides, if you feel my genes will provide a cure, why do I need the demon? I need to free my sister. Then maybe, we can find a way for me to help your people." She felt a sudden drive to get involved in the lives of a race she knew nothing about and make her mother proud. As long as Raven was safe, she saw no reason not to help.

"You need me for several reasons."

Ranata spun and faced Baal. "Why are you here?"

"I've come to apologize and to help you," he replied.

"I must go. Raven is safe presently, so you need to concentrate on the task at hand. Mate the demon, and find the cure." Chaval vanished, leaving her alone with Baal and her head spinning.

"Did he tell you?" Baal asked.

"About my mother?" Ranata headed out of the room. She hoped to put some distance between her and him but knew it would be futile.

"That and us?"

She faced him. "Yes, but why are you really here? You made it clear how you feel about me."

"No, it wasn't you. It was the fear of our son being a Sumari and having to kill him for it."

Her heart went out to him. When he'd mentioned them mating, it had never occurred to her that children would result. "I don't like the sound of that. Of any of this."

"I've since been assured that, when we decide to have kids, your human DNA will keep them from being Sumari." He stared at the photos on the bookcase. "When the gods decide they want a couple together, there isn't much arguing about it. You've heard of arranged marriages? This is no different."

"Whatever happened to love?" Maybe living in a fairytale and wishing for a prince to come riding up to whisk her away to a beautiful home was totally crazy. Then again, the world seemed totally crazy right now.

"Mated couples fall in love all the time." He faced her. "Is that what you want? For me to love you?"

Now, that was a million-dollar question. Did she? Hell, she didn't know anything about him other than he was a demon. "I just don't want you to hate me. This will be difficult enough without having that between us."

"I don't hate you, Ranata. You can't help what you are or your situation. It's simply that demon and fae are an unusual combination, and well...I wasn't ready for this."

Nothing about her situation was normal. "Chaval never explained why I need you. Do you know?"

He took a seat on the couch, arms spread across the back. "Because Hades decided we would make the best match. You need a mate who can protect you and give you the power you need to fuel your magic."

She felt her jaw drop. "Hades? As in..."

"Yes. The demon bastard himself." He leaned forward and rested his elbows on his thighs. "Look. I'll give you everything I possibly can. You'll have the finest home, the shiniest jewels and the best designer clothes. I'll lay down my life to protect you, and I'll teach you how to harness my power. Anything you desire will be yours, except I can never give you my love."

She wondered why his last declaration stung. "Is there another woman?"

"There was, but she died long ago."

"I'm sorry." *Great, so much for Prince Charming.* She turned to look out the window, unable to face him. "If I agree to this, maybe we can divorce after the cure is found, and then we can both go back to our own lives." She knew those golden eyes were staring at her.

"Love, I'm afraid it doesn't work that way. We mate, and it's for eternity. You'll become immortal, and you will lead your people. However, you can always choose to live in the fae realm without me. There's no law that says we must stay together, but you need to understand what the mating means before you agree."

She spun to face him. "Why should I care about people I don't even know. Give me one good reason I should become immortal and spend eternity with you?"

"For starters, to save your sister's life hopefully and because you can't let an entire race of people die. It's not in your nature." He snorted. "You and I will become the poster children for a fae-demon relationship. If you knew me, you'd find the humor in that."

Again, her mind went back to events leading up to now. Raven going missing, and now, living with a powerful lunatic. Demons on a killing spree, and finding out who she really was. As far as she was concerned, things couldn't get any crazier. She also had nothing left in this world. The only family she knew was missing. The tiny modest house she'd lived in was all that remained of her adopted parents. She had nothing to lose.

"Fine. I'll do it."

CHAPTER EIGHT

THE MINUTE he'd seen Ranata again, he knew he would follow Hades advice and mate with her. Not that he had a choice, unless he liked spending eternity having his skin peeled from his body then being burned to death only to be returned to life to repeat the process all over again. There could be worse fates than mating a beautiful woman. He only hoped she didn't decide to kill him in his sleep. Maybe, he should keep that little-known fact to himself because he was certain he'd piss her off enough to warrant his death.

"Raven's in serious danger, isn't she?"

"Yes. Eventually, Lowan will tire of her, and he will kill her. If he even suspects she carries fae blood, he won't hesitate to end her life. After all, he's the one who sent the virus running through the fae." He watched as she chewed her lip, and he found it damn sexy. He would enjoy his wedding night when he finally got this exotic beauty beneath him. However, it would be the last time he'd ever have a woman. Once mated, there would be no others, and it was likely Ranata would never have sex with him again. She was the type of woman who needed love, and he would never lie to her to gain her favor. He did have some morals.

"Am I supposed to destroy him?"

The thought of his mate going toe-to-toe with Lowan set him on edge. "No. I'm not even strong enough to take out Lowan. The Phoenix god is supposed to come back and take care of destroying Lowan, but that's another story. What you'll need to do is get your sister alone and snatch her. Something tells me she won't leave with you willingly. It's why you'll need to learn how to handle your power."

"Why can't you grab her? I mean...you're the demon with all the magic? Can't you simply kidnap her when she's away from him?"

He wished he could. "No. Seems fate has made its choice."

Resolve burned in her blue eyes. "Then I will do whatever I have to to save my sister."

"And does that include becoming mine?"

Her gaze narrowed to pinpoints. "Didn't I already agree? Besides, doesn't that mean you belong to me as well?"

He laughed. "I'm just making sure and yes." He shoved his hands into his pockets and rocked back on his heels. "You get all this for the low price of your mortality. Many women will be jealous of you. I mean...you'll live forever, frozen in the young, beautiful state you're in now and with a Kothar demon for a mate. I know many ways to please a woman."

Her cheeks flushed, and she rolled her eyes. "So now that we've established that, what happens next?"

"I see no reason to wait. We bond now then work on your power. However, I must tell you what the bonding entails. I will not have you calling foul later."

She nodded. "Seems fair."

Baal patted the couch. "Come sit." He waited until she'd settled in next to him. "First, I want to apologize for my actions earlier. I had promised to help you, and by telling you to leave, I broke that promise. I'm not proud of my actions, but I vow it will never happen again."

"I think I understand now. I know I have a lot to learn about your world, but human or immortal, no one wants to see their children die. I say we start over," she replied.

Beautiful and smart. Yes, Hades could have done worse. "That would be good. Now, we will have to go back to my home where I will perform the ceremony. I'll use magic to call upon higher powers to assist. First, I'll ask you if you give yourself freely to me, and when you agree, I'll leave my mark on your soul. Because you're not a demon and unable to perform the process in reverse, I will take a piece of you and mark myself."

She held up her hand. "Um, question. So, this marking of souls sounds painful as does the taking a piece of me. How bad will it hurt, and what exactly does it mean?"

"There will be no pain involved in our mating. The marking of souls will connect us. After, we'll have a link to each other. No matter where we are, as long as we allow the other in, we can communicate telepathically. I will know if you're ever in danger and will be at your side within seconds."

"Oh. Does this mean you'll be reading my mind?"

"Only if you allow it. I'll teach you how to communicate and block out others when you don't wish your thoughts to be known."

She seemed thoughtful for several seconds. "Okay. Continue, please."

"Once that's done, I'll have to end my life so you can become immortal."

Her eyes widened. "What? No. There was nothing said about you dying."

"Settle down. I'm immortal so, unless you chop off my head, I cannot stay dead."

She shook her head. "It sounds awful."

"It's not really. If you were a demon, it wouldn't be necessary, but because you're part mortal, I must make a sacrifice to give you immortality."

"I'm not stupid. Sacrifice means you're giving up something. Don't lie to me. What will really happen to you?"

He should have known from her history that she'd be concerned. "It will hurt like a motherfucker."

She scraped her teeth over her lip. "Is there no other way?"

Her concern touched him. *Don't let emotions rule. Fighting my feelings will be difficult enough once we bond.* Fuck, who was he kidding? Already, he was fighting instinct, and it made him crankier than hell. "None and I can deal with the pain. The last step to complete the bond is sex. I'm sorry, but it's required to seal the deal, so to speak."

This time, her gaze narrowed, and she glared at him. "You're sorry? Really? Why do I find that hard to believe? And, how do I know this isn't simply a way to get into my pants?"

"I admit I love sex. However, if we don't consummate the mating in twenty-four hours, it will reverse, and you will be back to where you started. Mortal. After our consummation, you'll never need to sleep with me again." Her scent—like a ripe Georgia peach on a dewy morning—made his mouth water. He wanted to kiss her but restrained himself. "Though...once you go demon, you never go back."

She shook her head. "Are you always such a smart ass?"

"Usually," he replied.

"This is serious, and why should I believe I have to sleep with you, again?"

"You'll have to trust me at some point."

She fisted her hands on her lap. "I did trust you once, and you let me down. Just know that I'll be on my guard from now on."

"I know I broke your trust, but I swear on my sister's life, I tell the truth. She's the one woman I love more than anything in this world."

RANATA HAD no idea why she should believe him, but she did. She wanted to hate the man who sat next to her, but it was evident he didn't want this any more than she did. The least she could do was suck it up.

"Fine. How soon can we get this over with?"

His body stiffened at her words. "We can go now, if you wish?"

"The sooner we do this, the faster I can get my sister back."

"We'll be on our way then." He stood, held out his hand, and she slipped hers into his. There was no way to miss the warmth of his skin, and it provided comfort as darkness swirled around her and pulled them into a void.

Seconds later, they appeared in a room lit by candles. Sconces hung on stone walls, and several dozen pillars formed a large circle around them. A small fire burned in the center.

"Where are we? This doesn't look like your penthouse."

"Hell."

She sucked in a breath. "What? I thought you were taking me to your home."

He chuckled. "This is my true home. Where did you think a demon would perform a ritual?"

"I guess I didn't think about that." She glanced around. "This looks like a room, not what I imagined Hell to look like."

He pulled off his T-shirt, and she tried not to gasp as the golden light bounced off his bronze skin. Shadows danced across the best set of abs she'd ever laid eyes on, and the lonely woman inside of her wanted to know what it would be like to experience one night with this man. Then there was the side that was frightened at the prospect. She'd have to shove that one down deep. Ranata would do anything to save her sister, including sleeping with a stranger. After all, it was only sex, and one didn't need to be in love to fulfill the body's desires.

But it would have been nice to fall in love and be loved in return. She shoved that thought aside, too. It was not to be her fate.

"There are different areas of Hell. Some are exactly what you imagine them to be. While others are very beautiful. This is a sacred place in Hades' castle where only matings are held. No one will disturb us here." He sat cross-legged on the floor. "I need you to sit here to my right." He patted the floor.

She complied and sat down cross-legged beside him.

Baal produced a dagger from thin air. The handle appeared to be of carved bone, but she couldn't see it well enough to get the details. She watched as he made a slice across his left palm, held it over the fire and let his blood drip into the flames. Every time a drop hit, the fire hissed and the flames turned a deep crimson.

"I call upon the power of the universe to bind my mate and I together for eternity. I willingly accept the pain of death to bring her immortality."

She cringed on the word *death*.

"Ranata, do you willingly accept me as your eternal mate?"

"Yes." She didn't hesitate, fearing if she took too much time to think about her actions, she'd realize how crazy this was. While she didn't fully understand the ritual, she knew it was far more than any human marriage would ever be.

He dipped two forefingers into the ash around the edge of the fire and traced something on her forehead. A strange sensation filled her as he continued a line down the bridge of her nose and to her lips where he stopped and applied light pressure. He chanted something under his breath, and her insides warmed. Feelings of contentment filled her, and she realized she'd never felt more alive. When he pulled his fingers away, he clutched the dagger with both hands and plunged it into his heart. She thought she'd been prepared, but let out a scream. Blood pumped from his wound with each heartbeat until he crumpled over in death, and she knew the image would be forever etched in her memory.

"Oh, my god." She scooted closer and tried to slow her racing heart. He'd instructed her that she'd have to remove the blade to finish the process. This was a demon's most vulnerable time. When they offered their immortality to another. She could choose to walk away and leave him, thus ensuring his real death, but where would that leave her? He'd placed a lot of trust in her that she wouldn't run, and she would not let him down.

With tears streaming down her cheeks, she gripped the bone handle and pulled the blade free then tossed it aside. She cradled his head in her lap and caressed his cheek.

"I'm so sorry you had to do this." Responsibility weighed heavy on her shoulders, but there was nothing to do now but wait. Neither of them had any idea how long it would take for his resurrection.

She wished for a cloth and water so she could wash the blood from him, and suddenly, a sponge and bucket appeared next to her. Without even questioning how, she dipped the sponge into the water then began the process of cleaning him up.

Time ticked by as she cleaned him up best she could. Her legs cramped from sitting on the floor, but she didn't move. The small discomfort she endured was nothing compared to what he had done for her.

Suddenly, his back arched, he opened his eyes then gasped right before he rolled to his side and into a fetal position. "Son of a bitch," he grunted.

She reached to touch him but hesitated. "Oh, god. What can I do?"

He clawed his way to his hands and knees. "N-nothing." He took in several ragged breaths. "Never take a knife to the heart. Stitching it back together is fucking painful."

She slapped her hand over her mouth. "I can't even imagine." She rushed to her feet and put her arms around his waist. "Let me help you." He straightened with her assistance.

"Thanks." He looked down at his chest. "How'd I get clean?"

"I managed to bring forth a sponge and water."

"Thanks again. I need a shower, and then we must finish the bond. We can go back to my penthouse or I have a home here."

"Here in Hell? I'd like to see it." Something told her she'd learn more about the demon in this environment rather than in a Las Vegas casino.

CHAPTER NINE

LUCAN ARRIVED in the most remote region of Hell. Being cursed, the guardians could no longer come to the Underworld without the stain on their soul growing at an alarming rate. Marcus had been here earlier, but only with the aid of the goddess, Qadira, who'd been able to keep the curse at bay and the darkness from growing, but he'd only had hours to accomplish saving his mate. Lucan, on the other hand, reveled in the darkness and as long as he stayed out of the bowels of Hell, he didn't seem to have any issues. He visited often, and every time he did, he caught the most beautiful voice singing. One would swear there was an angel trapped here, but he knew better. The place was full of deceit and trickery. Evil always tried to find a new means of escape so it could rain terror on innocents. Each time, he fought the urge to seek out the female behind the voice, but it was growing harder. He would never admit to his brethren that he came here just so he could hear her singing. Whenever he had the urge to do something dark and sinister, he sought out the voice, and it seemed to soothe him. For a short time anyway.

However, today, he wasn't in the pits of Hell to listen to the woman sing. He was searching for any clue that might lead to where

Lowan kept Chaval's sister. If she were freed, Lowan would no longer have control over the Sumari warrior, then maybe they could finally gain the leading edge. Having Chaval back on their side was far better than on the opposing team.

Lucan shifted into a thick black fog and floated along the ground. He'd have to enter the next level to begin his search. There, he could interrogate many of the demons who resided on that plane and hopefully find Willow.

Lucan? I sense you're here.

He halted. Never had the voice spoken directly to him. *Am I hallucinating?* Maybe he wanted to hear her so badly he'd conjured her?

I'm real, Lucan, and I need your help.

Who are you? As if he expected her to tell him the truth.

My name is Sabin, and I'm a prisoner here. Please...help me.

No fucking way was he getting dragged into whatever game she played. Prisoners were here for a reason. However...

I'm looking for a girl named Willow.

Why do you seek her?

He swore he detected jealousy in Sabin's voice. *She is a fae, and I have need of her. That is all you need to know.*

I have no idea where she is. Release me, and I will help you look for her.

Ah, so there was the deal she sought. *I cannot help you.* He formed a wall around his mind before she replied and tempted him further. He had a job to do, and chatting it up with some she-devil would only get him into trouble.

BAAL TOOK Ranata's hand and flashed them to his home. He had to admit, he'd been surprised when he'd opened his eyes to find her hovering over him. Not only had she kept her promise to remove the dagger, but she'd tended to him.

Don't let yourself get caught up in this mating business. It's only for convenience sake. Something told him he would be reminding himself of that often.

"It's not much, but it's home away from home. I haven't been here in several months."

Ranata walked across the modest living room and ran her finger over the bookshelf as she went. He hid a chuckle. He was one thing, and that was clean. He'd hired a demon to care for his place when he was away.

"A lake?" She stood at the large picture window with her hands on her slender waist.

"What? You didn't expect the Underworld to have water?"

She looked over her shoulder at him, her blue eyes blazing. "Not a freaking lake." She went back to gazing through the glass. "Or green rolling hills. Are you sure we're in Hell?"

"Oh, damn!" He smacked his forehead. "I knew I should have taken that right instead of a left at the fork in the road."

She looked back at him and laughed, and he realized he liked the sound. "Sorry. I just wasn't expecting this. It's beautiful." There was awe in her voice.

He stepped up beside her. "One of the perks of being Hades' favorite is I get prime real estate. This is the outer region of the Underworld. There are several layers to Hell, so to speak."

"Huh. So, will I be meeting Hades?"

"I'm sure he'll be by to make your acquaintance after we've completed the bonding."

Her body stiffened. Yeah, he didn't want to do it any more than she did, and he loved sex, but felt as though he were forcing her. "I'm going to shower," he grumbled and headed off to the master bath. After flipping on the water, he shed his jeans, kicked them aside and stepped under the spray. As he grabbed the bar of soap, he sensed another presence. He looked over his shoulder, and Ranata's curvy, naked body occupied the space behind him. She was totally bare, and she was glorious. His cock responded immediately.

"The soap please." She held out her hand, and he could do nothing but obey.

"You shouldn't be in here," he muttered, losing control of coherent thought.

She moved behind him then glided the bar across his back, and he had to bite his lip to keep from groaning aloud. Her fingertips traced a line down his spine, stopping at his tailbone.

"I realized I sent the wrong body language out there. I'm not in the habit of sleeping with men I hardly know, but it's been a very long time since I've felt a man's touch, and I must admit, I miss it."

At the rate she was going with her fingers and the soap, he'd have her pinned against the wall in a matter of seconds. Reminding her of what she had been missing. Instead, he dug for resolve. "I promise, you'll go away satisfied." He sucked in a breath and faced her. Water trickled across her breasts and down a well-toned stomach. Her full lips beckoned him as she flicked out her tongue and wet them further.

"I never doubted it for a moment." She soaped his chest.

"I want you to know I'm sorry about all of this." It irritated the shit out of him that this had been thrust on her. Even if she were taking it like a trooper, he was riddled with guilt that she was being forced into a bond with him. Granted, he hadn't been ready either, but he'd known the day would come eventually. She had been clueless her entire life.

She stared up at him with a look of confusion.

"I mean the mating, us...here...now. It's not fair that you didn't get to choose who you want to spend eternity with."

She smoothed soap across his abs downward, stopping at his pelvic bone. He placed his hands on her waist and, this time, didn't suppress his groan.

"You had no choice either. Did you?"

"No, but we grow up knowing that, one day, fate will decide who we'll spend our lives with. We watch mated friends and our siblings become happier than they've ever been. As much as we like to bitch, the gods have never made a bad match. On the rare occasions when things have gone badly, it's been because of free will. One of the chosen made a wrong choice."

"What do you mean?"

"Originally, Marcus was to mate with Aidyn's sister, but she wanted Drayos instead, and now, we have Lowan from that union." He stroked her cheek. "Sugar, you still have one last chance to back out of this. You still have free will." He swallowed. "You can run now, Ranata, and I won't stop you."

Her blue gaze bore into him, and for several long moments, she was quiet. "No. I'm sure you're familiar with the old human saying: when life hands you lemons?"

He nodded.

"Well, it's handed me a lot of them in my short time here, and I've always stepped up to the challenge. I wanted to believe God had a purpose for me." She laughed. "I had no idea it would be the God of the Underworld, but I accept it. My sister is all I have left, and I need her." She pressed her body into his. "We can make the best of this and become friends, or we can fight it and hate each other. I would much prefer the former."

If he were to be honest with himself, so would he.

STANDING naked in a shower with Baal felt surreal. Ranata had dug for her courage and decided to jump in with both feet. After all, if she looked at things logically, this would be the easy part of the tasks handed her. Rescuing her sister and saving a race of fae would be far harder. And in the end, she didn't want to hate him. It would only make them both bitter, and there had to be a better way. Even she understood eternity was a damn long time.

Besides, she would be stupid to deny she'd been attracted to him from the moment he'd walked into the bar that night looking for his friend. Had fate brought him there? She could certainly do worse for a husband. He was handsome as hell, and watching his cock thicken awakened her own arousal further. It had been a long time since she'd been with a man, and even then, she'd felt slighted. The guy had gotten his rocks off and left her hanging.

Need warmed her sex, and she pushed up on her toes, wrapping her arms around his neck. For a moment, fear that he'd reject her caused a lump in her throat, but it was shoved down when he brought his lips to hers. He was gentle at first, with only a peppering of light kisses, but with each one, he lingered a little longer. He swiped his tongue along the seam of her mouth, and she parted her lips until he swept inside. If she'd ever wondered what sin tasted like, she'd just found out. It was a mixture of dark chocolate and cayenne, and it heated her entire body with desire.

With every swipe of his tongue, her clit throbbed and begged for attention. She was almost ashamed of how badly she wanted him. Was this part of their growing bond or simply her body turned on from the lack of male attention? She slid her hand down the front of his chest until she'd made it to his cock where she fisted his length.

He broke the kiss and hissed. "We need to get out of this water." He reached for the handle and turned off the shower then grabbed a towel from the rack. "Allow me."

With tender care, he wiped the soft terry down her arms and across her stomach. He then knelt and dried her hips, thighs and calves. When complete, he placed a light kiss on her navel.

"Turn around," he whispered.

Somehow, she managed to get her shaky legs moving and offered him her backside. Again, he was gentle as he dried her back. When done, he tossed the towel then grabbed a fresh one and scrubbed it across his body in quick motions. Then he stepped into her, his hands rested on her hips as he began to kiss the nape of her neck and worked his way across the back of her shoulders.

She shivered.

"Are you chilled?"

"I... No." Far from it. Her body was on fire.

He gave a gentle squeeze to her hips and kissed his way down her spine. When he reached her tailbone, a kiss was planted on each cheek then she was suddenly lifted from her feet. She found herself in his strong arms as he carried her across the room and laid her on the bed.

"I smell your desire, Ranata." He leaned over and kissed between her breasts. "You will tell me if I do something that displeases you?"

She swallowed and wondered if that was even possible? "Of course."

He smirked. "Good." Then he latched onto her nipple. The swirling of his tongue over the hardened protrusion had her slipping her fingers into his thick black hair. It was even softer than she'd expected, and she wanted to bury her face in it. He moved to her other breast, and she arched her back into him and dug her fingers into his skull. When he released her, she almost cried out but noticed him smiling at her. Small, sharp points flashed at her.

"You have fangs?"

"They appear when aroused." He gave a slight shrug of his shoulder. "Or when pissed, but don't worry. I don't drink blood."

"Then why have them?"

"So, I can do this." He swirled his tongue across her nipple then bit down.

The bundle of nerves between her legs fired and sent a shockwave through her core. "Oh, my..." An orgasm took hold deep inside and carried her away. She would have expected pain from such an act, but this was far from it.

He smiled at her again. "Only the men of my species have them."

She'd hardly recovered when he licked her other nipple until it became so hard it was on the verge of painful, then he bit. Again, her body was flooded with pleasure beyond belief, and she experienced another orgasm. He released her and licked his way down her stomach, scraping his fangs along the way.

She dug her fingers into the sheets and pulled. A gasp escaped her lips.

"You are beautiful when you come, Ranata." He spread her legs and peppered kisses along her inner thigh, working his way to her sweet spot. Her heart beat against her chest, and she touched his forehead.

"I've never..."

He stopped and looked up at her, his eyes the color of burning embers. "No man has ever pleasured you this way?"

She felt her cheeks flush. "No. The last relationship was a bit one-sided." Now, she felt like a virgin.

"Then it's time to rectify that, love." He pressed his tongue to her cleft and swiped up to her clit.

"Oh, dear god."

It must have been all the encouragement he needed. He moved his tongue in circles. First slow then fast. Through her folds and then he dipped inside of her. She raised her hips to grind into him, and every nerve in her sex was on fire. Her breath caught in her lungs.

His fingers gripped her hips and held her firm as he pressed a fang into her clit.

Colored lights flashed, and she exploded. Was that her screaming? Impossible since she couldn't catch her breath. When she started to slip back down from the heavens, he slipped two fingers inside her and sent her skyrocketing again. Every muscle begged for mercy as her body went rigid for the second time, or was it the fourth. She'd lost count. If this was what it was like to be with a real man, she'd been missing out. Big time.

CHAPTER TEN

WATCHING Ranata glow from her passion gave Baal more pleasure than anything in his entire life. For a brief moment, he contemplated what it might be like to open his heart and fall in love with his mate. Fear had him shoving the thought away.

He placed one last kiss on the tender flesh between her legs then slid back up her body, positioning his cock at her entrance. "Are you ready, sugar?"

She licked her lips, never breaking eye contact with him. "Yes."

He slipped the tip in, tossed back his head and hissed. "So fucking hot." He thrust until he was buried to his balls and shuddered. The woman was on fire, and it pleased him immensely.

Grabbing her hips, he placed his arm under her, lifted for better access then began a slow, steady thrust. With his free hand, he brushed his thumb across her nub.

Her eyes widened. "Oh, god, not again."

He smiled. "You'll come until you've got nothing left to give." She'd be left completely and utterly sated, and he would be ingrained in her soul for eternity. He wanted her to remember him. Always.

Rocking his hips, he pushed his entire length until there was nothing left for her to take then used short quick thrusts. She was on the edge again, ready to fall any second, so he stopped.

"No. Don't stop."

He wasn't ready to let her have her way just yet, so he laid her back on the bed then leaned over her. Planting his lips on hers, he pushed at the seam of her mouth, and she opened. Their tongues danced together, and he consumed her, swiping and tasting every inch of her mouth. He kissed her as though he were a dying man, and this would be his last moment on earth.

She tasted like a sweet, succulent peach ready to be plucked. She pushed her fingers through his hair and moaned into his mouth. The bond between them was growing, and soon, there would be no going back. They would belong to each other for eternity. The thought scared the hell out of him. He'd lost the woman he loved long ago and vowed never to give his heart to another. Would he be able to protect Ranata and provide all she needed while keeping his heart intact? Better yet. Would he be able to let her walk away and choose her own life? One without him?

Damn it. He had to stop thinking and simply act on instinct. He'd been handed a duty, and he was expected to follow through.

Breaking from the kiss, he slipped free from the grip of her womanhood. "On your knees, sugar." She was quick to roll over and rise to her hands and knees, wiggling her beautiful ass in front of him.

"Damn fine," he growled and plunged deep, fingertips gripping her hips.

She mewled.

He leaned over her. "There's still time to change your mind," he whispered in her ear. Once he spent his seed inside her, the bond would be complete and unbreakable.

She turned her head to glance over her shoulder. "Not changing." Then she rocked her hips.

"Point taken." He kissed the base of her neck then sank in his fangs as he thrust in and out of her sex. Reaching under her, he rubbed his thumb across her clit, and she exploded into orgasm. Her hot, wet sheath tightened around him, and he couldn't hold out a second longer. His muscles contracted, and he filled her with his essence. He retracted his fangs.

HE CLUNG TO HER, unwilling to let go. She belonged to him now, and he to her. Their lives had been altered forever. A rush of emotion hit him, coming from her as she basked in the afterglow of her many orgasms.

Damn you, Hades. Baal already knew he'd lose his internal battle. How could he not fall in love with the woman to whom he'd just given a piece of his soul? He pulled free and rolled to his side, spooning her in next to him. "The bond is complete. I can hear your thoughts, so careful not to plot my demise," he chuckled.

"How do I turn them off?"

"Imagine building a wall of bricks. Place one at a time until you have a huge wall." He saw her mentally stacking blocks until he no longer heard her thoughts. "Good. You're a fast learner."

"It worked?"

"Yes, and you'll get so good at it you'll be able to build it and tear it down instantaneously. Now, reverse it, and break each brick down." He did the same so she'd experience his thoughts.

Well done.

"Oh, my god! I can hear you in my head."

Communicate with me. Simply think what you want to say.

This is so weird.

You'll get used to it. We can communicate no matter where we are.

You mean...we can be at opposite ends of the country?

Yes, and because a demon's bond is strong, we can even speak if we're in different realms. He felt a tinge of sadness that wasn't his. "What troubles you?"

"It's nothing. Just not how I thought my wedding day would be."

"I suspect you wanted the white dress and the whole nine yards?"

"What girl doesn't?" She turned her head and gave him a quick grin. "So where do we go from here?" She was quick to change the subject, but he knew she was disappointed in her fate, and he wished he could change it for her.

"Tomorrow, we head to the fae realm and see what we can find. Somehow, you need to connect with their doctors so they can try to find a cure." He rolled away from her and planted his feet on the floor. Already, he missed her warmth as he padded across the carpet to the closet. "I'll also begin your training. You need to learn how to protect yourself. For now, get some sleep."

"Where are you going?" her sleepy voice called.

"I have some things to tend to. Don't worry; I'll be back before you wake, you're safe here." He would never admit he was running. Already, the bond had him wanting to curl up next to her and take her several more times before morning came, but she needed time to adjust to this relationship. They both did. When he finally slipped out the bedroom door, she was fast asleep.

LUCAN, where the fuck are you?

Busy. Whatcha need, Seth? Lucan sat atop a hill overlooking a gully. Any moment, he expected a rush of condemned souls to enter, and the demons he wished to question would show up to begin their torture.

We're having a small gathering at Katie's. You up to coming?

A portal opened, and a dozen souls shot through. Things were about to heat up. *Sorry, bud, I can't leave right now. You understand how it is.*

Sure, I do.

He sensed Seth's disappointment and felt a twinge of guilt. His brethren were all he had left in the world. *I'm on a special mission for the demon, but what's up, brother? Do you need me? You know I will drop everything and come at once.* He owed Seth his life.

No, it's nothing like that. Katie and I were just going to announce she's pregnant.

No shit? Congrats, I'm happy for you both. As soon as I get back, we'll get together. Give her a hug from me.

Will do, and if you need my help with your mission, be sure to call on me. See you later then. Seth broke the link between them.

"Another baby." He shook his head in disbelief. Marcus and Cassie had been the first to bring the guardians a child and now Seth and Katie. Would miracles never cease? He'd like to think one day he'd be blessed with a son or daughter but often wondered if one as dark as he'd become would ever be given a mate.

Lucan? Why have you been ignoring me?

Listen, she-devil. I've got no time for you today. He snapped his mind shut before the female found her way back in again. He had to admit, he was intrigued by her, but what did she want with him? More important, why was she here? Would it hurt to find out?

He went back to looking out over the gully and watched the demons play with their new toys. He searched for one who showed signs of being uncertain. Lucan was the hunter, and the ghouls his prey. He would find the weakest one and pounce, like a wolf taking down a caribou.

He spotted one demon that held back, away from all the others. It was evident this was the one he wanted.

He shifted to a dark mist and let the heated winds carry him to his victim. He hovered slightly above the beast's head before he wrapped himself around its neck and squeezed.

I'm looking for a girl. Specifically, she would be a fae who is being held captive. What do you know of her?

The beast hissed. "Nothing."

You lie. You can either tell me or I'll take it from you.

"I swear I've never seen a fae."

Lucan sensed the demon's deceit and decided he'd no longer waste his time. He slipped into the demon's ear and entered its mind. God, he loved his gifts. The inky darkness of the evil swirled around him as he penetrated the demon's brain. Digging for images, he sought a female who would look different from a demon since he had no idea what Chaval's sister looked like. He knew she was full fae, so she would be different from her brother who was half-demon.

The beast screeched and twisted its head in pain, but Lucan refused to relent.

Should have told me what I wanted to know.

A fair-haired female came into view. She sat in a dimly lit room, but he could make out pointed ears peeking through her blonde hair.

Bingo.

RANATA OPENED HER EYES, stretched, then suddenly realized where she was. Sitting, she clutched the sheet to her chest and looked around. She was alone. Thinking back, she remembered Baal had left, but didn't recall him coming back. Was this how things would be between them now, or would they be able to bridge the gap? Her emotions were in turmoil, and she was having a hard time grasping that she wanted him. Not only sexually, but emotionally.

"Damn, it didn't take long for that bond to kick in." She threw her legs over the side of the bed and stood. Every muscle rebelled—mostly the ones she hadn't used in a while. A smile crept across her lips as she played out the details of last night. Baal had promised her pleasure, and boy, had he delivered. In spades.

Grabbing her clothes, she quickly dressed and slipped out the door.

"Hello?" The smell of bacon and coffee started her mouth watering.

"In here," Baal called out.

She followed the delicious aroma and found him standing in the kitchen cooking breakfast. The man wore only a pair of sweats, and she had to stop herself from staring at his naked chest.

"Don't you know the rule about frying bacon?"

He looked up from his pan. "Rule?"

"Yeah, wear a shirt." Though she had to admit it would be a shame to cover up such perfection.

He chuckled. "Grab some coffee and a seat. Breakfast is about ready."

She poured herself a cup of coffee and sat at the table. The kitchen was cozy in a small kind of way, yet modern. With stainless-steel appliances and black, tile floor, it certainly didn't lend itself to what one would consider a home in Hell. Then again, it wasn't as if she were an expert on the matter either.

"So, you said something about my training?" She grabbed some bacon from the platter he'd set in front of her, and a sudden rush of desire slammed into her. She met his gaze and realized it came from him. *Shit.* She tried to ignore it, because if she didn't, they would end up back in bed and fucking like rabbits for days.

"Yes." He scooped scrambled eggs onto her plate. "You need to learn how to fight. Unless I missed something when Hades...uh, filled me in on your past. You never had any martial arts training?"

She bit the bacon and chewed. "Hades told you about me?"

"Some. He thought it would be helpful in your training if I had a little background."

Why did she think there was more to it than that? "There was never any need for self-defense while living in the boonies. I can shoot, though."

He took the chair across from her. "Shooting's good. One of the benefits of now being immortal and my mate is your increased strength. How do you feel this morning?"

"Good. Now that you mention it, I feel energized." *And well fucked.* She tried not to blush but knew she was a failure.

The corner of his mouth twitched. "I'm glad you're feeling so...well."

Crap. Had he heard her thoughts? Or felt her desire as she had his? She needed to learn how to shut off all this stuff or she'd become distracted at the wrong time. Dipping her fork, she scooped up some egg and shoved it into her mouth.

They ate in silence, and when finished, she offered to clean up.

"Don't worry about it." He waved his hand, and the entire mess vanished, leaving a sparkling kitchen that looked as though it had never been used.

"You never cease to amaze me with the stuff you can do?" She tried not to relive last night, but it proved difficult, especially when he sat across from her. His black hair disheveled from sleep. Scruff darkening his jaw. She remembered it tickling her thighs. She caught herself licking her lips as she stared at his chest and studied every ripped muscle.

"Sugar?"

"Huh?" She jolted from her thoughts. *Oh shit! Did he notice me staring?*

I not only noticed, but I can hear your thoughts and feel your desires. "If you need me, Ranata, you only have to tell me. Last night, I gave you the chance to say no. Nothing has changed since then. I understand this relationship is harder for you to accept than it is for me. I will wait for you to come to me should you choose to."

She looked down at her plate for a moment, slightly embarrassed but only briefly. Lifting her head, she looked him in the eyes. "Thank you for allowing me the choice."

BAAL MEANT WHAT HE SAID. He would allow her to come to him if she desired, but he needed to get Ranata out of here and to the fae realm before he lost control. The damn bond was messing with his head, and he wasn't referring to the one on his shoulders, either. His fucking cock had gone rigid the minute she'd entered the room. He hoped that by leaving Hell, he might find reprieve.

"You're an idiot to think that," Hades snapped in his ear.

"Mother fuck." He spun to face the demon god. "Don't you believe in knocking?"

Hades shrugged. "No. I see no reason for it. Besides, it's not as if I caught you two going at it hot and heavy like newlyweds should be." He winked then walked toward Ranata. "Ah. So, you're Iris's daughter. You're a spitting image of your mother."

"You knew her?"

Baal snorted. "Ranata, this is Hades."

Her eyes widened. "Oh."

"Not what you were expecting?" the demon god inquired.

"Umm..."

Hades waved his hand in dismissal. "Don't worry, I'm used to humans believing I have red skin, horns and a tail." He stepped in closer, and Baal found himself fisting his hands. He didn't like another male being so close to his mate.

Deep breath, and remember, she doesn't really belong to you. This is only for convenience.

"Though I could shift to that foul-looking creature you all seem to think I look like if it would suit you better," Hades scoffed.

"No, no. I think you're very handsome."

Baal rolled his eyes. "Ranata, don't feed his ego."

Hades raised a black brow. "You should speak, *demon*." He turned his attention back to Ranata. "Now, my dear." He offered his arm. "Let me tell you about your mother. Would you like to see a picture of her?" Hades whisked her away before Baal could stop him.

"Well, fuck me!" He stormed from the room, realizing he followed his mate like a rutting male, and that darkened his mood further. When he finally caught up to them, Ranata sat on the throne to the right of Hades and stared at a photo he presumed was of her mother.

"She's beautiful. I wish I could have known her." A tear slid down her cheek and cut right through him. At that moment, he'd give anything to be able to reverse time and bring her mother back to her.

"Your mother loved you and your sister very much. It was why she hid you away." Hades slumped into his seat. "And why she begged me to give you a mate."

"I don't understand. I mean...I get the part about my blood being a possible cure, but how does being with Baal have anything to do with this?" She refused to make eye contact with Baal. Instead, she stared at Hades.

"His loyalty is beyond measure." He cast a glare at Baal. "Even when he questions my authority. His bravery borders on suicidal, especially when he goes nose-to-nose with Zarek, who happens to rule over all of us. You will encounter a lot of humans and immortals. Some will have your best interest at heart, while others will pretend to be loyal only to get what they want. Your mate will always be someone you can count on. He'll also be a stabilizer for your power, helping to keep you balanced. Otherwise, the human side of you will become ill when you're exposed to magic."

Her eyes widened. "That explains why I got sick all of a sudden."

"Yes."

This time, she looked right at Baal. "But by forcing us together, you've taken away the one thing that means the most in a relationship."

She'd just driven the knife deep and twisted.

Hades arched a dark brow then stared right at Baal. "I wouldn't be so sure about that."

CHAPTER ELEVEN

AS SHE STARED at the man to whom she was now forever bonded, sorrow filled her. He'd told her up front he could never give her his heart. At the time, she hadn't cared too much, but now, it bothered her. Was it their bond? All she ever wanted was the love of her real mother. It had eaten at her. Granted, her adopted parents had given her everything they could, and they'd loved both her and Raven. Still, she had felt betrayed, and now those feelings were once again upon her.

"Love isn't everything it's cracked up to be, Ranata," Baal said.

His words bit her like a sharp, freezing wind on exposed skin. She ignored him and turned back to Hades. "What next?"

"Now, I send the two of you to where your people are hiding. Hopefully, they can find a cure. The fae are needed in the war with Lowan."

"Where the fuck is the Phoenix god? Shouldn't he be awake by now and taking care of our problem?" Baal ground out.

Hades sighed. "These things take time, and we need all hands to fight until he awakens."

"Who's the Phoenix god?" Every time she turned around, there was something new to learn.

"Long story, but he's the only one who can kill Lowan," Baal stated.

"Uh, not exactly."

They both turned to stare at Hades.

"What?" Baal's jaw tightened.

"He can't kill Lowan, either. You know…the whole god rule and how we're not allowed to smite one of our own? However, his power will send Lowan back to confinement. Another is destined to kill him."

A low rumble began, and Ranata looked to see where it came from. It didn't take her long to discover it actually came from Baal. He stood erect, fists at his side and eyes blood red. She swore horns had emerged from the top of his head.

"I think you have some explaining to do."

Hades jumped from his seat and stormed toward the demon. Suddenly, Ranata feared for Baal's safety. "Please, no fighting. I'm sure there's an explanation." She had no clue what was going on, but a deep need to protect her mate surfaced.

The god towered over Baal. "Do not take that attitude with me. Is it my fault all of you misunderstood?"

"Son of a bitch. So, do you intend to spill?" Baal pushed out his chest and stepped in closer to Hades. Ranata chewed her nails.

"I can only tell you that there's another who will be strong enough to kill Lowan. She only needs to be released from her prison and willing to plunge the dagger of Embara into his heart," Hades replied.

"You bastard. We are nothing but pawns in your games." Baal's temple visibly throbbed. Ranata stepped closer, fearing one of them would strike the other down.

"Hades, who is this woman?" Ranata decided she was either brave as hell or stupid. She went with stupid because she didn't feel a bit courageous at the moment.

Baal turned her way and scowled. "Ranata, you need to back the fuck away."

It was her turn to flash a dirty look at him. "Don't get snippy with me."

"I'm done with both of you." Hades waved his hand, and darkness surrounded her. The air was so black she couldn't see her hand in front of her face.

"Baal?"

Several seconds ticked by with no reply, and she panicked until the veil around her suddenly parted to reveal a pale-blue sky with splashes of lavender and pink.

"That rotten bastard," Baal growled beside her. "And what's with this hot and cold shit from you?"

"What are you talking about?"

"Earlier you said you accepted this relationship and wanted to be friends. Then just a bit ago you mentioned love. I thought you understood I can never give you my heart. Ever."

She pulled back her shoulders and pretended his statement didn't bother her. "Look, I said we should be friends, and I meant it. Yes, it would be nice to have a marriage of love and happiness instead of the one being forced on us." She shoved her hair out of her eyes. "We've performed the bonding. Do whatever's required of you then you can go back to whoring about." She turned to walk away, but he grabbed her and pulled her to him.

"When a demon bonds, their desire for any other is gone." A glint sparked in his eyes. "There's only you, sugar, and you need not worry that you'll have to sleep with me again. Unless, of course, you feel the heat of arousal between your legs, then I'd be happy to put out your fire."

She wanted to wipe the smirk off his face. "Really? Do tell. Does the female's desire for other men wane, as well?" Why had she traveled that route? Only moments ago, they'd been having a lovely breakfast, and he'd given her the choice to come to him on her terms.

Now, they quarreled like a couple—well, a couple forced into marriage.

He cupped her chin. "You're playing with fire by even mentioning another man. I'm a bonded male, and should you ever decide to seek out another man's attention, I will kill him. Test me on this only if you want another's death on your hands. I gave you the chance to flee, and you chose to stay. You belong to me now. Be satisfied that I will not make demands as is my right." He released her, turned then walked away.

What had she gotten into? And, why did she suddenly feel abandoned?

BAAL HAD EXPECTED a slap across the cheek, but instead, Ranata only glared at him. He turned and walked away, knowing she'd eventually follow. They were in a foreign land. She had no choice.

"You know, we've all had a broken heart at some point in our life." She stepped in next to him. "You need to learn to let go."

He refused to look at her because she was right. "Do you have blood on your hands because of it?"

Shock registered on her face. "No. Are you saying you caused her death?"

"She took her life because of me. I should never have fallen in love with her."

Ranata stopped and placed a hand on his arm. Damn it, she was supposed to be pissed at him. He knew how to deal with that, but her compassion melted away his reserves, and he wasn't ready to surrender to the bond completely. If she were angry then he could keep his emotions under control.

"It isn't your fault she chose to die instead of live. I'm sorry though that you had to go through that. No one should, but isn't it time to let go?"

"You need to understand the bond we have. It's a connection, like soul mates, and it means we are loyal, protective and seek to meet the other's needs. Whether it is a need for food, shelter or sexual fulfillment. Love usually comes as the couple spends time together, but it can be turned off."

"So, are you saying you can both hate me and have a need to protect me at the same time?"

Now was his time to make a choice. How he answered her would determine the type of future they would have together. He could harden his heart totally and become a demanding mate, bending her to his will. Or, he could give her what she desperately seemed to want.

"Do you know what it's like to have the woman you love slip away in your arms, and nothing you do, no one you beg, will save her?" He still felt Beth as she went limp against him after confessing to taking poison. Her heart had stilled, and his had shattered.

Ranata shook her head.

"I will never hate you, and as I promised before I will give you all that you need. It pains me that I can't promise you love, but know this: your demise would cause me great pain because we are connected. If I were to give you my heart and you left me... It would kill me. I'm not ready to take the risk. I'm truly sorry."

She touched his cheek and surprised the hell out of him. "No, I'm the one who's sorry. I didn't mean to stir up painful memories. We will take this one day at a time," she whispered.

Damn it. Again, his resolve was tested. "Your people are hiding here. Let's go find them."

IT BOTHERED her that he hurt, and she had to wonder if their bond created the turmoil she carried inside her as well. It wasn't like her to care so much about a stranger's feelings. Then again, she supposed she couldn't consider him that since they had already been through a lot. After all, he'd rescued her from a fate worse than death then basically married her. *And let's not forget the mind-blowing sex.* She blushed every time she thought about it. The urge to have him take her fast and hard right there on the ground caused her to bite her lip. Somehow, she needed to tamp down her overactive sex drive. Or maybe not. Would it be so bad if they met each other's needs? Could they have a relationship based on mutual respect and understanding? Maybe, with time, his wounds would heal once he realized she would never do anything to hurt him.

As they approached the top of a ridge and looked out, several people mounted on horseback greeted them. They all dismounted and quickly dropped to bended knee on the ground before her.

"Well, Your Highness, seems your people await you," Baal stated.

Ranata snapped her jaw shut and watched in disbelief as a handsome man with long blond hair approached her. He bent at the waist in a bow.

"Your Highness. On behalf of our people, I welcome you home." He straightened. "I am Heremon, and I will be your personal guard." His blue eyes flashed. "It is a pleasure to have you here finally, and may I say, you look just like our beloved queen."

She needed to find her tongue before she looked like an idiot in front of all these people.

Sugar, deep breath. You'll be fine. Baal managed to slip into her mind and offer comfort.

"Thank you. I'm happy to be here." She extended her hand and hoped it was the correct thing to do. *No one schooled me on the protocol for this sort of thing,* she shot back.

He chuckled. *You're the queen. It's whatever you want it to be.* He stepped closer to her side and folded his arms over his expansive chest. "And just so we're clear, *I* am the queen's personal guard, and I wish to inspect your warriors."

Heremon shot up a brow. "Demon. While we appreciate your escorting our queen home, this is fae territory, and you should do well to remember that."

Baal leaned forward. "And you will do well to realize I don't give a shit, and Ranata is mine. I'm sure you've learned in your lifetime what happens when you get between a demon and his mate?"

She should be pissed that he claimed her, but not only was it reassuring to have him by her side as her protector, it was damn sexy.

"You, *Demon*, should have been around long enough to know you're in over your head here. We can use your power to destroy you."

"And I will die protecting her. You must realize she is safest with me," Baal growled.

Ranata sighed. She was in a foreign land, with magical beings and no clue what to expect. Time to test the waters. "Enough of this pissing contest." She pulled back her shoulders and pinned a glare on Heremon. "You will direct all matters of my safety to my mate." Turning to Baal. "And you will play nice."

The look of surprise on both male's faces had her feeling pretty proud of herself. She'd just put two superpowers in their place. "Now, can we get on with our duties?"

The guard bowed. "Of course, Your Highness. I apologize for my rudeness and promise it will never happen again." He moved his attention to Baal. "I have a mount ready for the queen if you care to inspect it."

Baal held up a hand. "No need. I trust your judgment."

The other man nodded. "This way then." He led them across a grassy field to where the others waited.

Thank you for toning it down. She hoped Baal heard her.

I only did it for you, and I'll sense if anything is wrong with your mount. However, be warned. One step out of line by any of these fae, and I swear to Hades, I will rip this place to shreds. Your safety is my only priority.

Noted.

She allowed Baal to help her into the saddle and pretended she knew what she was doing. She'd ridden a couple of times when she was younger, but that had been several years ago. Her sophomore year in high school to be exact, when she'd had a serious crush on the boy down the road. Jake's family had had several horses so she'd agreed to go riding with him, wanting to make an impression. They used to ride every Sunday after church during nicer weather. He'd take her up into the mountains, and she'd pretend not to be scared shitless every time the horse would stumble slightly. It had been worth it, though. As time went on, they'd fallen in love, and one sunny afternoon, she'd lost her virginity to him. The two had always talked about the future and planned to marry one day and have a couple of kids.

Jake's family moved to Germany the following year when his father's company transferred him. They had both been heartbroken and written frequently, but after a time, the letters had come less often, and then one day, Jake had broken her heart. He confessed he'd been seeing someone else and had gotten her pregnant. He was married and a father at the young age of eighteen.

Shall I hunt down this Jake and make him hurt, sugar?

She jolted from her thoughts. She hadn't even realized they were moving. Now, she looked to Baal, who rode beside her. "Why are you in my head? Some things are private."

"Then you should keep your mind closed." He stared straight ahead. "I'm sorry he broke your heart."

"It was long ago. I'm over it."

"Huh. I sense a little sarcasm there," he replied.

She couldn't stop the smile that curled her lips upward. "Perhaps."

They'd just come to the top of a ridge when Heremon moved up beside them. "Your Highness, below is our new home. It took a lot of magic, but I think you'll find it to your liking."

When she looked into the valley, she spotted a large castle and several small cottages dotting the landscape around it. *Really? This looks like something from the Dark Ages.* She dared not voice her opinion aloud, fearing she'd offend Heremon.

Get used to it, but don't be deceived. The fae have their quirks, but they also like modern conveniences. You'll find it very pleasant on the inside, Baal responded.

"Very impressive, Heremon. I cannot wait to see it."

The guard seemed pleased. "Shall we then? I know the doctors are most anxious to meet with you and begin finding a cure for the virus."

"As am I," she replied and wondered if it would be rude to make a hasty exit after a cure was found. She needed to get to Raven.

CHAPTER TWELVE

LUCAN SHIFTED BACK to human form and watched the demon writhing on the ground in pain, drool running down the beast's chin. "Be thankful I allowed you to live," he snarled then flashed to just outside the location where he'd seen Chaval's sister.

Lowan would have the place laced with traps and heavy magic. How the hell Lucan would get in was another concern. As he stood outside the stone mansion, he contemplated the risks. He could see the woven magic surrounding the building and wasn't so stupid to think he could penetrate it.

He shifted back into the mist and skirted the perimeter. Following the dark magic, he looked for any opening, no matter how small that might allow him in.

Nothing.

The place was locked down tight, and he had no way to break through.

I know how to get in.

Damn it all to hell. *She-devil, how'd you get back in my head?*

I have my ways. Help me, and I will tell you how to get in and rescue the girl.

He was getting tired of this woman and the pull she had over him. It was like playing a game of Russian roulette, and at any minute a bullet would lodge in his head. There was no denying she was a temptation.

I know your dark secrets, and if you help me, I will submit myself to you.

He shifted again and fisted his hands. There was no way she could be referring to what he hoped she was. *I have no idea what you mean.*

You know exactly what I mean. Your sexual preference of subduing your female when you take her. I will give you what you want. I only ask that the first time you are gentle as I am a virgin.

What the ever-loving fuck? He wiped sweat from his brow. A virgin willing to submit herself to his dark side? The thought had his cock thickening and pressing against his jeans. His heart raced, and hyperventilation loomed. He needed to calm his ass down before he lost total control and agreed to anything she offered.

I cannot trust you. You refuse to tell me who you are.

You will not be able to resist me forever, Lucan. Soon, your darkness will force you to succumb to me. You'll release me, and I will kneel naked at your feet.

Lucan swallowed and opened a portal. He needed to make a hasty exit and figure out another way to rescue the fae.

AFTER A SHOWER and a change of clothes, Ranata settled into her suite and curled up on the sectional sofa. "You were right. Looking at the outside of this place, I never would have expected such luxuries."

"Glad you like your rooms. I'll sleep on the couch, so you needn't worry," Baal stated. "I'm going to inspect the warriors, but I'll be back in time for dinner."

"I'm sure we can get you your own suite. There's no reason for you to sleep on the couch." In reality, she wanted him to stay close. Being in this strange world made her uncomfortable, and Baal was quickly becoming the one constant in her life.

"I don't want any of these people talking about us not sleeping together. At least behind this closed door, they have no idea and can assume we're acting like any mated couple would. To lead them to believe otherwise might cause problems." He strapped a dagger to his thigh. "I trust no one right now, not until they prove themselves loyal."

"I guess that makes sense. Well, Heremon should be here soon to take me to the lab for blood draws. When can we begin my training? I'm itching to get to Raven." She felt as though she'd been neglecting her sister, but luckily, the fae had kept tabs on Raven and reported she was still alive and well.

"If you feel even the slightest bit uncomfortable, you reach out to me immediately. Understand?" The look on his face told her she wasn't to argue, and she was relieved he was on her side.

"I will."

"Good. Tomorrow, we'll begin your training and readying you for rescuing your sister. Don't forget, you also need to convince the fae their help is needed."

"I know." There was a knock at the door, and Baal flung it open to reveal Heremon on the other side. The fae bowed.

"Your Highness. I've come to take you to the lab."

"Right." She jumped up and walked to the door, and as she neared Baal, he snaked out his arm and pulled her to his chest. His mouth found hers and crushed.

Consumed.

Burned and ignited a fire so hot and deep inside her she swore it would burn her alive. When he released her, his eyes burned with desire, and she had to wonder if it had been a show for the man next to them or if it had been real.

"Take care of my love, Heremon."

Then, Baal walked out, and she realized he'd only been trying to convince the fae. She touched her lips. A tinge of sadness that he hadn't meant it blanketed her. However, the emotion was quickly replaced by something else. In that moment, Ranata was determined to win his heart.

BAAL STRODE AWAY with a smile on his face, but panic hid just under the surface. Yeah, he'd kissed Ranata to put on a show for the nosy bastard, Heremon. He'd enjoyed it too and was eagerly awaiting when he could feel his mate beneath him again. Being the one responsible for her cries of pleasure made him smile wider. Yeah, his resolve was quickly melting.

He took the stairs down to the ground level then exited through a side door. He headed for the large, stone building housing the fae guards.

Would it be so bad to open up to her? After all, they would be together for eternity. He liked Ranata. The woman was beyond sexy, but not only that, she was smart, compassionate, and determined. Those were qualities he would have sought if he were choosing a mate for himself. The woman had him rattled and unable to think of anything but her.

Not stopping to knock, he swung open the door and strode into the common room. Several fae looked up from their cups of brew and stared at him. Okay, maybe he was stupid for barging into their space. Relations between the species had always been strained, but better to establish his leadership now. He marched to the center of the room and took a stance, crossing his arms.

"I'm the queen's mate and will relish gutting each and every one of you with a dull knife should you let a hair on her head come to harm. Do we have an understanding?"

They all blinked then the one in front rose. "I'm Kalin, the commanding officer. My men and I will protect the queen with our lives."

Baal snorted. "You'll pardon me if I remain a bit skeptical since Iris is now dead."

Kalin's features darkened. "The one who failed to protect the queen has since been slain by my hand. It will not happen again, but it is our hope that Iris's daughter will bring the cure to our plague."

Already, Baal liked this Kalin and sensed his sincerity. "May we speak privately?"

The fae nodded. "Follow me." Grabbing a bottle from the table, the commander made his way down a long corridor with Baal on his heels. The fae led him through a door into a simple office with a heavy, wooden desk, a table scattered with prints and a couch. Walking to the desk, Kalin opened a drawer and pulled out two shot glasses, filling each halfway with amber liquid from the bottle he'd snatched.

He offered one to Baal, who graciously accepted.

"You have some big balls to walk into a room full of fae and start making demands," Kalin pointed out.

He shrugged. "You know how mated males are."

Kalin snorted. "Stupid from what I've seen."

"Maybe, but it worked."

"True. You knew it would gain respect from the men."

He'd hoped that would be the case and raised his glass. "To your queen."

The fae raised his. "To the queen." They both tossed back the fiery liquid.

Baal wiped his mouth. "I want you to train Ranata in your ways. Make sure she knows how to harness the power of others and use it to protect herself."

Kalin refilled the glasses. "That duty falls to Heremon."

"I don't trust him."

"And you do me?" Kalin raised a black brow.

"You know demons have a sixth sense, so to speak. Yes, I trust you. Ranata wants to rescue her sister, and we will help her." He'd already delved into the fae's mind and gotten everything he needed.

The man in front of him smiled. "I love a good fight. I will begin her training tomorrow, and you will be the conduit?"

It was Baal's turn to grin. "I will give her all she can handle."

The fae's features turned more serious. "I hope the cure is found quickly. Several of our people have become afflicted with the virus. If we're discovered, it could prove fatal. Half of my warriors have come down with the fucking thing." He swirled his drink then tossed it back.

"Have your doctors any idea how long it will take?"

"None, but they are positive the queen's blood will work. In the meanwhile, we continue to hide like a bunch of cowards."

"Not cowards. It is a smart thing to do until this is resolved. Until then, you have me." Baal was matter-of-fact.

Kalin set down his glass. "You are that powerful?" he whispered.

"Between you and me, I am the most powerful Kothar demon alive. Keep that in mind when you're training my mate."

"If this is true, why have I never heard of you?"

"Not many know, and I like to keep it that way, but I figured you'll discover what I'm capable of as soon as you tap into my magic."

Kalin poured another round. "I look forward to finding out."

RANATA QUICKLY REGAINED HER COMPOSURE. "Heremon, lead the way."

The fae tipped his head and swept his arm outward. "This way, Your Highness. This shouldn't take long, as they only need to draw a couple vials of blood."

"Good." There was something about Heremon that caused her concern, but she couldn't put her finger on it. Not that he'd done anything. It was simply intuition that said to watch her back around him.

She tried to pay close attention to her surroundings. Her suite was on the third level of the castle and took up the entire floor. The second and ground levels were reserved for those in charge of the army, such as Heremon and a few others she'd yet to meet. The idea was to place them between the queen and any possible threats that might enter the front door. She had to question how well that idea worked since she'd only recently learned the entire story of how her mother had been killed. She'd bring up the subject with Baal later.

"The infirmary and lab are just off the west wing," Heremon said and led her through a set of lead-glass doors and across a white, marble floor. She found all the luxuries a bit over the top and much preferred Baal's humble home in Hell.

She chuckled.

"Something funny, Your Highness?"

"Sorry. Just a personal thought."

He grunted. "Here we are." He led her into a room filled with stainless steel and bright lights. Two people in white lab coats occupied the space, and both turned to greet them, giving Ranata a bow. She threw on her best smile though she hated all the formality.

"Your Highness, may I introduce Wendell and his mate, Thalia."

Ranata held out her hand. "I'm pleased to meet you. I certainly hope you can find a cure for this virus."

"We believe we'll be successful," Thalia replied. "Your Highness, please come take a seat, and we'll get you out of here as fast as possible." She escorted Ranata to a chair, and Wendell went back to what he'd been doing.

Thalia smiled as she tied a rubber tourniquet just above Ranata's right elbow. She couldn't help noticing how beautiful the fae was. Long, red hair curled to her shoulders and bright, green eyes complemented her smooth, creamy skin. She was perfect, just like all the immortals Ranata had come across. For a moment, she felt a pang of jealousy just thinking of all the women Baal had likely been with in his life. She suddenly realized she had no idea how old he was, and for some stupid reason, she needed to know. As she watched her blood fill the vial, she wondered what this bond to him really meant. She'd had no one other than him to talk to about it. He'd mentioned having a sister, but she hadn't yet met the woman. Maybe, he didn't want them to meet.

"All done." Thalia's voice broke through Ranata's thoughts, and Ranata realized they were alone. Wendell had disappeared.

"Oh, that was fast. What happens next?"

The fae walked to the counter and placed the vials in a centrifuge. "Now, we make a serum and test it. If successful, we should know within twenty-four hours after the vaccine is administered." She turned and smiled. "May I speak freely?"

The inquiry took Ranata by surprise until she remembered these people looked at her as royalty. "Of course. Please."

"I'm so sorry about your mother. I know it must be difficult for you, being thrown into this. Did you have any idea who you were?"

"None. I grew up thinking my real mother had abandoned my sister and me."

Thalia shook her head, and her red curls danced around her face. "Iris was my best friend." She wiped away a tear. "She loved you and had planned to come for you, but then she became ill." She went to a drawer, pulled a set of keys from her pocket and unlocked it. She reached inside then came back with a small, white package. "She wanted you to have this." Thalia rolled a stool in front of Ranata and handed her the box.

Opening it, Ranata was stunned to find a silver, heart-shaped locket. When she pulled it out and pressed the little button to pop it open, she sobbed. A photo of her mother holding a tiny baby, a small child seated next to her, was mounted inside. "Is that Raven and me?"

"Yes. She wore that every day, and when she became ill, she gave it to me for safekeeping." She looked around, as if to make sure no one was around. "She also wanted me to tell you why she went to Hades and begged him to mate you with a demon."

"Why? Why did she think it necessary to marry me off?"

"She wanted you safe and protected and knew a demon wouldn't contract the virus. Matter-of-fact, so far, it seems the demon race has been the only one not cursed by Lowan or his father. I suspect it might be impossible since they share DNA."

"Thank you." Ranata placed the locket around her neck, and just then, the door swung open and Heremon stuck his head inside.

"All done, Your Highness?"

She tried to hide her disappointment at being unable to ask more questions now. She'd simply have to pay Thalia a visit later.

CHAPTER THIRTEEN

BAAL HAD STAYED with Kalin longer than he should have, but he'd left feeling confident the fae commander was the right choice to train his mate. *My mate.* He laughed. He'd never thought he would be saying those words.

He crept through the front door of their suite, where only a small lamp still burned on a side table in the living area. Trying to tiptoe his way to the couch, so as not to wake Ranata, he cringed when the floor groaned under his weight. Hopefully, she was fast asleep and wouldn't hear him come in. He would just curl up on the couch. Except there was one small problem. She was sleeping in his spot.

Kicking off his boots, he made his way toward her and admired how her dark hair curled around her cheek then fanned out over her shoulder. He watched her breathe. Her chest rose and fell, and he saw the pink tips of her nipples pushing into the thin tank she wore. He licked his lips, wanting to pull the hard buds into his mouth and make her moan. The bond pulled at him, and he caught himself digging his nails into his palms as his gaze moved to her naked thighs and down her calves. Had she meant to torture him with her state of half-dress?

Deep breath. He'd have to carry her to bed. There was no way he'd let her sleep all cramped up on the couch when she had a perfectly comfortable mattress in the other room. He reached down and scooped her up, pulling her close to his chest.

She stirred.

"You're back," she whispered and threw her arms around his neck then laid her head on his chest. He took in the scent of her coconut shampoo and wished they were alone on a sandy beach. He walked to the master suite. With one arm, he pulled the covers back and gently laid her down. When he went to pull away, she groaned.

"No. Stay here tonight. I don't want to be alone."

He swallowed. Did she mean it or was it sleep talking? It was hard for him to discern, and he worried what the repercussions might be if he made the wrong decision.

"You don't really want me to sleep in the same bed, do you?"

She opened her eyes. "I wouldn't have said anything if I didn't mean it."

"Are you okay?" He sat on the edge of the bed and worried. "Did something happen at the lab? You didn't call for me."

"I met a woman named Thalia. She was my mother's best friend, and she gave me this locket." She fondled a silver heart that occupied a spot between her breasts. He wondered how he'd missed it before. "Am I selfish because I wish I could have known her?"

"No, sugar." He pulled off his tee and tossed it to the floor then unsnapped his jeans and pushed them down. After stepping out of them, he slipped into bed next to her and pulled her close to his chest. "It's perfectly normal to want your parents to be here with you." He kissed the top of her head and wished he could ease her pain.

"Thalia said my mother chose a demon because she wanted me protected and because you wouldn't get the virus." She tipped her head back and looked up at him. "Thanks. I know I've not been the easiest to deal with, but thank you for being here."

He ran his thumb across her cheek. "You're welcome."

She let out a soft chuckle. "Not like you had a choice, though. I'm sorry about that, too."

"Neither of us had a say in the matter, but we will make the best of it." He meant it, too—the part about making the best of it. Ranata continually impressed him with her constant drive and ability to adapt. With what had been thrown at her, it was to be expected. He was proud to call her his.

"Do you realize that you're the only friend I have in this crazy mess?"

His chest tightened. He'd seen her entire life through Hades' gift, but now, that she mentioned it, unless she was with her sister, she'd usually been alone. "Shh, you need to get some rest. You have a big day ahead of you tomorrow." Tomorrow, he'd call on Lileta. His sister would be pissed at him as it was because he hadn't introduced her to his mate sooner.

He stroked Ranata's hair as she slept against him and tried not to think about his erection. He promised to allow her to take the lead in the sexual department, something he hadn't done since Beth. Usually, he simply turned on his charm and seduced any woman he wanted. He could do that with Ranata, too, and it wouldn't take much since she was mated to him. However, for the first time in many years, his conscience kicked in, and he was desperate for Ranata to want him. All of him.

RANATA SAT up abruptly and looked around. Sun filtered in through the sheers over the windows, and the spot next to her was empty. She remembered falling back asleep on Baal's chest after asking him to stay with her.

She ran her fingers through her tangled hair. "Crap. What must he think of me?" Just then, he strode through the doorway wearing only a pair of jeans and carrying a tray. She had to admit she would never grow tired of seeing him half-dressed. The man was a sight that stirred a firestorm between her thighs.

"Morning." He set the tray on the bed. "Breakfast. You need your energy." He snapped open a linen napkin and laid it across her lap.

"Wow. Did you get the staff to do this for you?" She eyed the bacon, eggs, flapjacks and orange juice.

"I'm crushed. I cooked this myself."

She sipped the juice. "Thank you, but why would you go to all that trouble?"

"Why would I not? Get used to being spoiled," he replied and sat in the chair beside the bed.

She wasn't sure what to think, and this whole mate process confused her. She wished she had someone to ask. She supposed she could talk to Thalia, but she wasn't sure how much the fae knew about demons. She dove into her breakfast.

"My sister will be coming today. She's been dying to meet you, and Lileta will also be a good one to aid in your training." He picked a bottle of perfume off the vanity next to him and sniffed. "Ew, please don't wear this stuff." He wrinkled his nose and pretended to gag.

She giggled. "I promise. I thought it was only me who hated the smell. I can't wait to meet your sister. Do you think we'll get along?"

He snorted. "Are you kidding? Lileta can give you some great advice on handling a mating not of your choosing. She's mated to a dragon shifter, found out her father is Lowan and has sailed through like a trooper."

Ranata looked up from her bacon and couldn't help but smile. It was obvious he loved his sister deeply. "Sounds like we need to bond over a daiquiri or something."

"Right." He stood. "Hurry up and finish eating then get dressed. You've got twenty minutes." He was out the door before she could respond. She hurried and chowed down her breakfast then headed for a quick shower. The entire time her mind tried to wrap itself around Baal serving her breakfast in bed. He'd made it himself, too, and to her, that was something you did when you cared for a person. It gave her a warm feeling inside. Maybe, there was hope for him after all. She hated that he'd lived with a broken heart for so long. No one should ever suffer like that.

After a quick shower, she braided her wet hair, threw on a pair of jeans and a tank top then exited the bedroom. When she ran into the living room, she saw Baal speaking with a stunning woman. Her hair the same dark color as his, and when she turned to face Ranata, she had the same golden eyes.

"Ah, here she is," he said.

The girl gave her a huge smile and rushed forward. "Hi, I'm Lileta, and I'm so happy to meet you at last." She pulled Ranata into an embrace.

"I'm so glad to meet you," Ranata replied.

The girls separated. "We'll talk more after your training today. I'm anxious to help however I can."

"Thank you. I'm ready, I think. What do we do next?" She was anxious to begin the next phase so she could concentrate on Raven.

"Let's go. We're meeting Kalin in the courtyard in five minutes." Baal moved to the door.

"Kalin?" Ranata followed on his heels.

"Yes, I met with him last night and checked him out. I trust him to do a good job and watch over you when I'm not here. Heremon... I don't like."

Funny, neither did she, so they were starting the day in agreement. "I trust your judgment."

Baal gave her a nod and a smile then held out his hand to her. She accepted and welcomed the warmth of his touch.

I need you to keep your mind open to me today while you train. You'll use me as your conduit for power. He squeezed her hand. *Make me proud, and kick some ass today.*

She took in a steady breath. *I'll do my best.* Failure wasn't something Ranata was used to. She'd always pushed herself to excel at everything she did, and this would be no different. Raven was depending on her and so was her mother. She tried not to think about the fact an entire race of people did, as well. That was simply too much.

When they entered the courtyard, they were greeted by a fae she assumed must be Kalin. He wore black jeans and a dark tee, and his raven hair was tied back. The man cut a lethal appearance, and his green eyes flashed with determination. For a moment, Ranata worried whether or not he was on their side until he stepped forward and bowed.

"Your Highness, I am Kalin and at your service."

"Hello, I'm pleased to meet you. I understand you'll be training me on how to fight?"

He smiled. "When we finish, you'll be considered a lethal weapon."

She laughed. "I think I like the sound of that." She rubbed her hands together. "Just tell me what I need to do."

"First, I'll teach you how to detect magic then how to harness its power for your own purpose."

"Okay." It sounded complicated.

"The best way to learn is to close your eyes," he continued, and she complied. "Good. Now, shut everything else out of your mind and concentrate only on the darkness in front of you."

Considering it was relatively quiet, she didn't have much trouble blocking out the background noise and staring at the backs of her lids.

"Everything black?" Kalin asked.

"Yes."

"Okay. Now, look for any light, no matter how faint or small."

"You mean like spots?"

"Perhaps. It looks different to each of us. Tell me what you see."

She tried not to fidget. "I see blue blotches. Kinda. I think."

He cleared his throat. "Look at me, Your Highness."

She popped open her eyes and stared into his green ones.

"I'm asking permission to address you by your birth name. May I?"

"Of course. I hate the formality anyway," she said.

"Ranata, while we are in training, you're considered my pupil and I will hold rank over you. Anything I do or say is for your own good and the safety of your person. You will not hold it against me either now or later. Acceptable?"

"Um, I'm not sure what you're asking me?" Now, she felt like a complete idiot.

Sugar, he wants to make sure you don't decide to have him assassinated later for anything he does or says here now. Tell him you grant him clemency.

Oh crap! What the hell is he going to do to me?

Don't worry, he will not harm you. I would never let that happen.

She swore he growled, but it must have been her imagination. "I grant you clemency."

"Good. Ranata, there is no *kinda* or you *think* when it comes to these exercises. Either you see the light or you don't. Now, try again, and this time pretend your life depends on it."

She closed her eyes and tried to relax. "Yes, I see faint blue light. It looks like a clothesline snapping in the wind."

"Much better," Kalin replied. "Now, grab hold of it and give it a jerk. Feel its energy pulsing in your fingertips."

Ranata mentally took hold of the line, and when she touched it, she suddenly felt as if she could take on the world.

You are a natural, sugar. Now, kick some ass.

She opened her eyes and smiled at her mate. This might actually be fun.

CHAPTER FOURTEEN

LUCAN FLASHED BACK to a small cabin he'd purchased a couple years ago. It was tucked on the shores of a remote lake in the mountains of Romania, and he often came here when he wished to be alone. Lately, that seemed like most of the time. That wretched witch in Hell was getting to him. She was all he could think about, and now thanks to her, he had visions of her blindfolded, bound and naked. At his mercy and ready for him to take what he wanted. He desperately needed that.

He wondered what she looked like. Blonde? Brunette? Did she have long hair that flowed down her back and was made for wrapping in a man's fist as he fucked the hell out of her? His fangs lengthened at the thought. It had been a long time since he'd had a woman. He left human females alone for fear of hurting them, and when he became too desperate, he found a willing Kothar demon to sate his urges.

"Damn that wicked bitch." He walked to the water's edge and looked out over the lake that reflected back like a mirror in the midday sun. "Why does this female tamper with my mind?" He raked his fingers through his hair. He needed to cool off so he could think straight and deflate his erection.

Grabbing the hem of his tee, he pulled it over his head and tossed it to the ground. Unbuttoning his jeans, he toed off his boots then shoved the denim down his legs. A breeze blew and tickled the hair on the back of his legs.

He shifted into mist, the form that allowed him so much freedom and let the warm air carry him high above the rippling water. When he reached a satisfactory position, he shifted back. Stretched out his arms, straightened his body and sped like a bullet toward the lake. Upon impact, he broke the water's surface and shot to the bottom, navigating better than the local otters who often joined him for early morning swims. The coolness of the lake invigorated him and made him feel alive again. Something he lacked on most days.

He touched the bottom then pushed off to head back to the top. When he broke through, he took in a deep breath and turned his face to the sun. A lonely howl greeted him. He shielded his eyes and looked to the shore.

"Kaldaka." He kicked and began to swim toward the huge, black wolf. He'd come across the beast three years prior, wandering alone in his neck of the mountains, and they'd bonded instantly. Lucan had blessed him with the name Kaldaka, meaning *wolf* in his native language of Draconic. Since that time, they'd sat many nights high up in the mountains and watched the moon dance across the sky.

Lucan reached the shore and gave the wolf a scratch on the top of his massive head. "How are you today, boy?"

Kaldaka responded with a whine and a wag of his tail then looked to the thicket of trees to the west. Lucan followed his gaze but saw nothing.

The wolf let out a bark.

"What's bothering you?" Suddenly, he scented another, and it was then a beautiful silver female came into the clearing and trotted their way.

"You dog. You've found yourself a mate and a beauty at that," he whispered. Kaldaka shot off and greeted the female with a lick on the face then ran and circled her, making his way back to Lucan.

He laughed. "I think she gets the idea." Both wolves moved toward him, and the female pushed her nose into the air and sniffed. Lucan dropped to his knees and held out his hand. "Come to me." Her amber eyes stared at him then she moved forward without hesitation. Unlike with humans, they had nothing to fear from him.

She pushed her head into his hand, and he stroked her soft fur. "I will call you Vor. It means *beauty* in my language." She seemed to like his choice because she licked his hand, and it was then he sensed the stir of pups. He cast a glance to Kaldaka. "Damn boy, you didn't waste any time. Can't say as I blame you." Already, the female was several weeks along with her litter. Lucan was elated for his canine friend and sad. Everyone around him was finding happiness, and all he could do was continue his fight to keep from slipping completely into the darkness.

"I'd better get dressed. I've got a fae to rescue." He rose and gathered his clothes then turned toward the house. "I don't suppose you have any suggestions?" he asked Kaldaka. The wolf responded with a bark, and Lucan laughed. "I didn't think so." He reached down and scratched Kaldaka's ear. "Take care of your mate, my friend. She is the most precious thing on earth." He stepped onto the porch and watched the two wolves run and frolic their way back into the woods.

With a sigh, he went inside to change. When the sun set, he'd search for Jax. Maybe the Draki could help him get to Chaval's sister.

BAAL SENT out a burst of power but kept it gentle enough that Ranata could handle it. Kalin proved an excellent teacher, and as expected, his mate was an exceptional learner. Already, she'd managed to harness some of his magic and flash herself from one end of the fae realm to the other. Next was to open a portal into another realm. Once she succeeded in doing that, she could go anywhere at any time.

"You can do it, Ranata," Lileta yelled from the sidelines, ever the cheerleader. He was thankful she'd come today. It was evident having another female here had helped Ranata relax.

With a flash of light, a portal opened. Kalin wasted no time dragging Ranata through, snapping it shut behind them. All was quiet now, and it was the perfect time to take care of something he needed to do.

"Lileta, I need to tend to something. Will you let the others know I'll be back shortly?" He hoped so anyway.

"Sure. What are you up to?" She jumped up from her seat and approached.

"I have a surprise I'm working on for Ranata."

Her brow shot up. "Is my brother's heart beginning to melt?"

"You're crazy."

She punched him in the arm. "Not. I can read you like a book, though, and my sixth sense tells me you can't resist her. Stop fighting what's natural for a mated couple." She palmed his cheek. "She will fall in love with you and hard. Don't break her heart."

"You know that is not my intention." Now, he was curious. "Why do you think she'll fall in love with me?"

"I have a woman's sense, and I can see what you can't. It's happening already." She shrugged. "And I have a good friend who can see the future." She winked. "Now, go knock your mate's socks off."

Baal flashed. He knew his sister referred to Gwen, the female guardian with the gift of soothsaying. She'd seen the other guardian's mates in a vision. Had she seen Ranata? He wondered why she'd never told him.

This time, he'd flashed himself to Zarek's front door instead of inside. He hated eating crow, but he needed to do this, and only the king of gods could grant this wish.

The door swung open, and the god's wife, Qadira, greeted him.

Her messy, flaming-red hair and flushed face spoke volumes. "Demon. How pleasant to see you. How is Hades?"

"He's well, I guess," he replied and dropped to his knees. "I seek an audience with your husband."

The corner of her mouth turned up. "Damn. This must be important for you—"

"How dare you darken my doorstep again?" Zarek roared out from behind his wife and tried to move her away. The woman wasn't budging. "Wife, remove yourself while I kill me a demon."

If the statement were meant to frighten Baal, it didn't work. Lucky for him, the goddess had always had a soft spot for him.

"Zarek. You will not harm one hair on his head." She pointed her index finger at him. "And don't take what I'm saying literally or you won't get laid for a century." It was apparent she knew her husband would look for any loophole to get away with slaying Baal.

"Damn it, woman. Fine!"

"I'll be listening for sounds of murder." She pinned him with a glare then seemed satisfied and walked away.

Zarek's fangs grew longer. "What. Do. You. Want?" The god stared down at him.

"Look. I know I'm disrespectful and all that, but for fuck sake, I'm on my damn knees. I don't even kneel before Hades unless he makes me. Don't take my dislike personally. It's just how I roll."

The god sighed. "Why are you such an ass?"

Baal shrugged. "You guys are always sticking your noses where they don't belong. Except when we really need your help, then you're making up rules as to why you can't interfere. I should be asking you why you're such an ass."

"Children learn from their mistakes. Believe what you will, but it's not always easy to look the other way when you're fucking up." He waved his hand for Baal to get up then brushed past. "You may not believe it, but when Iris came to me for help, I sent her to Hades and told her he had the perfect mate for her daughter."

Baal stepped beside the god who stared into the bottom of a fountain. "Are you trying to say you knew he would pick me?"

"I did, and for all your disobedience, you are loyal." He faced Baal. "I am sorry for not saving Beth, but she wasn't destined to be in your future."

Baal was at a loss for words. He'd never expected Zarek to apologize for ignoring his plea to help Beth. "It didn't mean she had to die."

"She would have never moved on without you."

"You could have at least saved Beth and erased her memories of me," Baal growled.

"Then your lesson would have been void. Sometimes, we must hurt, we must bleed and we must sacrifice. Watching the woman you love die was yours. It was what made you into the rebel you are, into one who will bend to no one's will. You're a powerful demon who will protect those he loves with his very life. How many times have you sacrificed yourself to save another?"

"I don't really know." It wasn't something he'd considered.

"Far too many to count. It's not a common trait in a demon. Hell..." Zarek laughed. "Not even I can break a will that strong. Now, what is it I can grant you?"

Baal wasn't sure what to think of the conversation, but he was here to ask for a favor, and he'd take full advantage of the god's current good humor. "I would like to grant Ranata a visit with her mother."

"Holy hell. Now, I never saw that one coming," Zarek exclaimed. "You realize what's involved?"

"Yes." Always a sacrifice, as if he hadn't given enough already.

"Very well then. It would seem your heart isn't so cold after all."

"YOU'VE DONE WELL TODAY, Ranata. Learning more than I'd hoped. Tomorrow, we'll begin again," Kalin said as he walked her to the door. "Have a restful evening, Your Highness."

"Thank you." Ranata had learned to flash, open portals and even steal magic. She was exhausted and also a bit surprised she hadn't gotten ill once. Apparently, the bond with Baal had not only made her stronger but dampened her human weakness to magic.

She slipped into her suite and headed for the shower, noting Baal had been missing for some time. Lileta had said he'd gone to take care of some business, and she wondered what he was doing. Pulling off her shirt, she remembered the kiss he'd given her only yesterday and how he'd pulled her into his arms last night.

She slipped her jeans down her thighs and walked the rest of the way to the bathroom in only her underwear.

"What a nice vision to come home to."

She spun and faced Baal. "I didn't hear you come in."

"I didn't use the door."

Which meant he'd flashed in. "I've gotten pretty good at popping in and out myself." She couldn't help but smile with pride.

"I heard. I spoke with Kalin before I came in. He gave me a glowing report." The demon's eyes sparkled with mischief or was that desire? She'd forgotten she was standing in her bra and panties.

"I was just going to shower."

He grinned and arched a brow. "Is that so?"

"Um, yeah." An idea struck her. "Would you like to come wash my back?" Suddenly, she feared he would reject her.

He responded by pulling his shirt over his head and gifting her with a magnificent view. "I was hoping you'd invite me." He stepped forward and held out his hand. She accepted, and he led her to the shower.

Reaching in, he flipped on the water, and four shower heads came to life, wetting the black tile. He slipped one strap of her bra off her shoulder then planted a kiss at the nape of her neck. Repeated the process with the other strap then reached around and unhooked the fabric, sliding the bra off he tossed it to the floor.

He traced his fingertips up her back then pulled her to him. "You are a beautiful woman, Ranata," he whispered then brushed a kiss across her lips. "Are you sure you desire this?"

Christ, if she hadn't, she sure as hell did now. To say he was gifted at seduction would be an understatement. "I'm sure, but I have a question." Oh, why the hell was she going down this road?

"I'll do my best to answer. What's bothering you?"

She swallowed and prayed this didn't backfire and make him angry. "When Heremon came to pick me up, you kissed me before I left. That wasn't just any normal kiss, Baal. Did you feel the need to put on a show for him?"

"You mean like this?" His grip around her waist tightened, and his mouth slanted over hers. She opened, and his tongue swept in, sliding across hers. Dominating. Demanding. Giving no mercy. Not that she wanted any. His erection pressed against her belly and heated every inch of her body.

He slowed. Pulled back slightly, taking her bottom lip between his teeth as he broke away. She found herself holding her breath and grappling for control of her senses. It was a losing battle. She looked up at him. His eyes burned like molten copper.

"Y-yes. Why do you kiss me like that?"

He grinned. "Because I desire to. Doesn't it please you?"

Dear god in heaven. She would lose herself to him. Heart, body and soul. She was already on the downward spiral.

"Ranata? Have I done something wrong?"

"No, but that's the problem. You do everything right, and yet, I'm expected to keep my heart out of this relationship." She had to look away. "I'm not sure I can do that anymore."

He touched her chin and forced her to look at him. "What are you saying?"

Her pulse sped up from the fear of telling him, but it was best to keep things out in the open. "I'm saying that as hard as I'm trying not to, I'm falling for you. I'm sorry."

He brushed his thumb across her cheekbone. "Don't be sorry."

He kissed her forehead. "We are mated, our souls are combined and your feeling's only natural."

She laced her arms around his neck and touched her lips to his. She wanted to scream that if the feelings were natural, why did he refuse to return them? Instead, she pleaded, "Just please don't break my heart."

"I'd never intentionally hurt you."

The fire that burned inside her was stoked even hotter. She wanted him. Here. Now. She reached for the button on his jeans. She yanked at it then pulled down the zipper, shoving his pants to the floor. Wrapping her hand around his cock as best she could, she stroked it.

He moaned. "We're streaming up the bathroom, sugar."

"Is that a bad thing?" The shower was still running.

"Not in my world."

"Good. I'm not in the mood to stop what I'm doing because of a little steam." She rubbed her thumb across the tip.

"Damn, woman. I've a mind to bend you over the counter and have my way," he growled.

She'd just reached the boiling point. "Don't make threats unless you intend to follow through."

Before she knew what was happening, he grabbed the waistband of her panties and yanked them away from her body, then moved her backward until her ass hit the cool slab of stone.

"Turn around and place your hands on the counter," he commanded. His gaze narrow and dark.

She obeyed as heat flooded her sex, and her chest rose with rapid breaths. She swallowed, her mouth like cotton in anticipation of his touch. The feel of his heated hands on her hips caused her to squirm.

"I need you," she whispered.

"Do you now?" He slid his palms along her ass cheeks, stopping to give a squeeze. He pushed his knee between her legs. "Spread farther."

Again, she obeyed, rather liking the bossy side of him and hoping it would prompt him to hurry and scratch her itch. She was fast rewarded with the tip of his cock sliding along her seam before he gripped her hips again and pulled her to him.

She gasped as her nails raked the marble surface. Stretched and filled completely, she wanted to stop time so she could enjoy this one moment just a little longer. However, when he began to slide in and out, she nearly came undone. Looking into the mirror in front of her, she watched his reflection. His eyes were closed, and small fangs peeked out from his upper lip.

God, he was sexy, and he was hers.

He rocked faster. The sound of flesh slapping flesh and their passionate moans echoed in the steam-filled room.

"Come for me." He reached around and brushed his thumb across her clit.

Every nerve pulled tight then snapped, sending her into an orgasm that weakened her knees. She only remained standing because of his hold on her hips.

He hollered out as he drove into her and arched his back. "Damn."

After a few moments, he leaned forward, his arms around her waist. Their gazes met in the mirror then something strange happened. Ranata became overwhelmed with emotion but realized it didn't come from her. There was something in his eyes, and she couldn't explain it, but it was raw and primal and then it was gone along with the feelings that had bombarded her.

Had something just passed between them?

CHAPTER FIFTEEN

LUCAN PROWLED the dark alley and wrinkled his nose at the stench. "Fucking filthy demons." He kicked an empty whiskey bottle out of his way then stopped to listen.

He heard a grunt up ahead.

Flashing, he was just in time to witness Jax take off a demon's head with the flick of his clawed hand. The demon's head landed and rolled, stopping on Lucan's boot. "Damn it, Jax." He kicked the object of his disgust out of the way. "These were new boots yesterday."

The Draki shrugged. "Teach you to wear your Sunday best to a killin' spree."

Lucan grunted and walked to where Jax stood. "I need your help. I've located Chaval's sister, but the magic around her is so tight I can't get through." Dragons were notorious for their ability to find a weakness in any magic spell.

Jax slapped his hands together and rubbed. "Please tell me we're going to Hell?"

He shook his head. "You're as twisted as I am."

The shifter laughed. "Lead the way."

Lucan opened a portal then shifted and shot through. Jax, in his dragon form, was hot on his tail. It didn't take long for them to reach the desired destination since Lucan now knew where he was going. He just hoped that fucking bitch stayed out of his head.

He circled the area where the magic was woven around the prison containing Willow.

Here. Can you see it? He'd slipped into Jax's mind.

I can. Give me a little time to study it, and I'll get us in. Jax soared off, and Lucan shifted back.

You've come back, and I see you've brought back-up this time.

"Son of a bitch," he swore under his breath. Why couldn't she leave him alone? He would just ignore her and hope she went away.

I'm not leaving you alone until you free me.

Damn it, woman! I'm not setting your wretched soul loose on the world. Leave me be.

Lucan. You need me. The world needs me. She began to sob. *I've been alone for so long.*

Great. Just what he needed. A mind fuck. *Your tears will not work on me.* He hated it when a woman cried.

Jax, hurry the fuck up!

Christ, Vampire, settle down. I've found a weak spot, but get ready. Shit's gonna hit the fan.

Bring it.

Anything would be a welcome reprieve to the female in his head. Even being outnumbered by demons. He swung his arm into the air and brought back his favorite sword.

A loud roar permeated the thick air just as the magic around the prison came tumbling down. Jax flew by and dipped a wing. Lucan was happy to have the bronze dragon on his side. Not only was he good at magic, but Jax was a star warrior. One of the best the Draki had, which was good because the thing charging at him was ten feet tall, had one large eye in the center of his head and was uglier than shit.

SHIT. Baal hadn't meant to let his guard down, but he had, and now, all he could do was pretend it didn't happen. As long as Ranata didn't bring it up, everything would be fine. He'd shove his feelings for her back into the deep abyss. Back where it was safe.

Easier said than done. He'd grown a damn conscience, and now, the fucking thing was talking to him. He'd ignore that, too.

Pulling Ranata closer to him, he pressed his waking erection against her backside. "I have a surprise for you."

"You do?" She flipped over, so she faced him. Even better.

"I've arranged for you to go to the Temple of the Gods."

She sat up, concern marring her beautiful face. "Why?"

"Zarek has agreed to allow access to your mother. You'll have one hour with her." He played with a strand of her hair, curling it around his finger.

Her jaw dropped. "I don't understand. How is that possible?"

"When immortals pass, they go to another realm. Usually, there isn't contact with them once this occurs. However, a powerful god can allow a brief meeting between our world and theirs. They just have to agree to do it."

"I-I can't believe this. Why would Zarek do this?"

"Because I asked him."

Her gaze pinched down, and she stared at him. "Why do I feel like there is more to this than you simply asking for a favor?"

He brushed his fingers up and down her arm. "It was exactly that. You'll see your mother in a few hours, but as I said, time is limited, so you cannot be late. I'll drop you off, but Kalin will see you back. It will be good practice for you. Opening portals, that is."

She lay back again and snuggled into him, but he sensed she still didn't believe him. "Why is Kalin bringing me back and not you?"

"I have some business to tend to, and I trust Kalin."

"I guess I'd better take that shower now." She rolled out of bed.

"I'd offer to wash your back, but I'm afraid I'd only detain you,"

Baal laughed, missing the warmth of her next to him. He wanted to stay with her. Have her one more time before he had to endure his week of Zarek's torture. The thought of being away from her, leaving her without his protection, had him grinding his teeth. That alone was torture. However, he had to trust Zarek and Hades' promise to keep her safe while he was gone. He understood the penalty he had to pay for his request. It didn't mean he had to like it, but he would endure his suffering. Which reminded him...

He jumped from the bed and quickly dressed then stuck his head into the bathroom. "Ranata, love. I'll be back in a few minutes. I need to pay a visit to an old friend." He flashed before she could reply.

Baal narrowed his eyes on his intended victim, who still lay in bed asleep. He focused and entered the man's mind then delved through all the darkness. Being a demon, he recognized the stain of evil on the bastard's gray matter. He flipped through Clive's memories and replayed the night he'd attacked Ranata. He felt himself shift, his demonic state becoming more apparent as he watched through Clive's memories as he tore Ranata's clothes. The man's intentions clear.

Baal wanted to slice him open and spread his entrails across the room. Except, that would kill him, and Baal had other plans.

Grabbing Clive by the foot, Baal jerked him from the bed. "Wake up, you little shit. Your nightmare is about to begin." This asshole was going to pay.

Clive opened his eyes and focused on Baal. "What the hell? Who are you, and how'd you get in?"

"I understand you like to snatch innocent women and sacrifice them. You wanted to summon a demon? Well, motherfucker, you've got one." He flicked his wrist, using magic to lift Clive first to his feet, then dropped him to his knees.

"Fuck, man, I think you broke my kneecaps," Clive cried out.

"Tsk, tsk. Man up, you little prick. Should have thought a little harder before you touched Ranata or her sister," Baal growled then grabbed Clive by his collar and brought him to his feet. He threw a punch that landed square on Clive's jaw. If Baal hadn't been holding the human by his shirt, he would have knocked the man across the room.

Clive managed a laugh, blood spraying from his mouth. "Those bitches? They both got what was coming to them. What are you anyway? Satan's lackey?"

Baal wrapped his hand around Clive's throat and let his claws dig into the man's skin until blood flowed. Baal wanted to choke the life out of him, but that would be too easy. Instead, he pulled Clive closer. He let his fangs lengthen for effect and watched the piece of shit in his grip squirm. "I am Hades' right-hand demon, and one of those bitches—as you called them—happens to be my mate. You're double fucked since the other is her sister whom you've handed over to Lowan. I'd like to kill you here and now, but the thought of you spending eternity in Hell sounds more fitting." He grinned. "After all, you wanted a demon. Now, you can have hundreds."

He summoned a portal and dragged a kicking Clive inside.

Seconds later, they appeared before Hades, who waited on his throne. Baal hid a smile. The god had brought out his pet serpents and allowed them to slither around. "So, this is the human who caused so much trouble?"

"Yes." Baal gave a shove, pushing Clive to the floor. "Clive, meet the Lord of the Underworld."

Clive clawed his way to the throne and pawed at Hades' leg. "I'm your humble servant."

Hades laughed. "Yes, you are." Then he kicked Clive backward. "You are responsible for letting Lowan escape his confinement here by sacrificing a virgin. You also laid an angry hand on a demon's mate and meant to rape her. You're not fit to lick my boots."

"I wasn't going to touch her! I swear!"

"Silence! You'll speak only when I command it." Hades flicked his wrist, and Clive's mouth was sewn shut. The pathetic human moaned and pawed at his lips to no avail.

Baal chuckled.

"The punishment for your crimes is eternity in purgatory. You shall know unquenchable hunger and thirst. I also have a few sex-deprived demons who will love to make you their bitch while they feast on your flesh." He leaned forward. "Over and over and over again."

Clive shook his head. Muffled screams came from his sealed mouth as he scrambled up and tried to run. He didn't get far before he vanished. No doubt sent straight to his prison.

Hades grinned. "Some days, I love being the Lord around this place. Today is one of them. He will suffer for what he has done. You showed excellent restraint by not killing him yourself."

"I wanted to but realized his punishment with you would be far worse." He shrugged. "Besides, I plan to visit him often."

"He is your prisoner to do with as you wish." Hades' expression grew serious. "Take care with Zarek today. Remember your training, and you will survive your sacrifice intact. Did you tell Ranata of your fate?"

"No. She only knows I asked for her mother to visit. She needs to concentrate on her training, not the fact I'm being tortured for my request. Only Kalin and Lileta know where I will be." He'd sworn them both to secrecy. If Ranata found out he had bargained with the god for Ranata's access to her mother, it would upset her greatly. He didn't want her to feel responsible for his torture.

"How will you explain your absence? Your wounds when you return?" Hades inquired.

"I'll figure it out. I need to go. It's time for me to take Ranata for her visit." He flashed before Hades could stop him.

RANATA HAD SHOWERED and dressed in record time and now sat on the couch, legs crossed, tapping her fingers on her knee. What the hell would she talk to her mother about?

Baal flashed into the room, and Ranata jumped a foot.

"Damn, you scared me."

"I sense you're nervous."

She rolled her eyes. "Ya think? I haven't seen my mother since I was a young child, and now, I get to see her ghost and I've got one hour to make up for a lifetime of questions."

He slid in next to her and put his arm around her shoulder, pulling her close. She leaned into his hard body and felt her tension melt away. It was then she realized how much she relied on him. He was like a security blanket, making her feel warm and comforted.

"Can you stay there with me?"

He kissed the top of her head. "I wish I could, but duty calls. I have some good news, though. I've just spoken with Kalin, and it appears the vaccine is working."

She lifted her head. "Really?"

"Yep. The half dozen they've tested it on are no longer showing signs of the virus. They plan to inoculate everyone today." He tipped her chin up and gave her a kiss, lingering only for a moment. "You can tell your mother it was a success."

Her eyes teared up. "I guess I can. I wish I could tell her I have Raven, safe and sound."

"You will. Soon." He stood and helped her to her feet. "Ready?"

Her heart pounded until she thought she might faint. She took a deep breath. "Yes." She needed to get her shit together.

"Come here." Baal pulled her to him and wrapped his arms around her, holding her tight. *You'll be fine. Keep your mind open, and reach for me if you need me.*

Next thing she realized, they stood on a stone path in the center of a beautiful courtyard. Fountains splashed water over colored-glass stones, and the sun warmed her skin. She glanced around and saw several large buildings with tall, marble columns. Everything looked bigger than life.

"What is this place?"

"Temple of the Gods. Each god or goddess has their own home here. The large one at the top of the hill belongs to Zarek." He laced his fingers with hers. "We'll walk the rest of the way so you can enjoy the beauty."

They started up the stone path, and she noted how everything seemed brighter here. The colors were more vibrant than she'd ever seen. Flowers bloomed along the path and filled the air with their fragrance. Women milled about, dressed in white, flowing garments, reminding her of ancient Greece.

"It's beautiful here. I feel so out of place, though." Just then a tall man appeared in front of them. He looked slightly out of place, wearing faded jeans and a black Pink Floyd tee. His dark hair was tied back from his face and accented his silver eyes. He was gorgeous.

He bent at the waist. "Your Highness, welcome to my home. I am Zarek, and may I say you are as stunning as your mother."

"Thank you." How she'd managed to speak without stuttering amazed her. As she understood it, the king of the gods had just bowed to her and addressed her by title. *Holy shit.*

He grinned. "And why would I not address you as such? You are the rightful queen of the fae and your position is to be respected. Never forget it."

Her mouth dropped open.

"Zarek can read all thoughts. Nothing is sacred around him, no matter how hard you try," Baal interjected.

Zarek flashed him a scowl, and for a moment, Ranata feared for her demon, but the god's expression changed. "Be thankful, demon. Your mate seems fond of you. However, it is time for you to leave."

Baal vanished without a word.

"You haven't hurt him, have you?"

"No, my dear. Shall we? Your mother is waiting." He offered his arm, and for a brief moment, she thought of calling the entire thing off, but then placed her hand on his bicep.

"Yes." The scenery in front of her blurred then came back into focus. Except it was different. They stood inside a small courtyard, surrounded by crimson bushes. A single fountain, with a snow-white statue of a woman cradling a baby to her bosom, commanded attention in the center. Off to the side was a long table, and trays of food covered its surface. At one end, a woman rose from her seat. She wore a long, red gown that draped off one shoulder. Her hair was black as night and fell in large curls to her buttocks, pointed ears peeked through it. But, it was the large, blue eyes that looked at Ranata and filled with wonder and love that caused her to choke up. A tear slid down the woman's cheek.

"I will leave you ladies alone." Zarek bent closer to her ear. "Remember you have an hour. The clock in the center of the table will begin once I leave." Then he was gone.

Ranata willed her legs to move, but they refused. She couldn't believe her mother, the woman who had birthed her, stood in front of her. No, she was gliding toward Ranata as graceful as a swan on a calm lake.

"Daughter." The woman held her arms wide, and Ranata couldn't take it any longer. The little girl who'd ached for her mom broke into tears and ran into her mother's arms.

Iris squeezed her and rubbed her back. "Shh. I'm here now. I cannot begin to tell you how sorry I am that I was unable to come back for you and your sister."

Oh, god, she had to tell her mother that Raven was in danger. She had failed to take care of her baby sister.

Her mom held her at arm's length. "You have never been a failure. Where Raven is now was never your fault and is beyond your control." She stepped to the side and slipped her arm around Ranata's shoulders then led them to the table. "Sit. We have much to discuss and little time."

CHAPTER SIXTEEN

BAAL FOUND himself in the one place considered hell for a demon. A frigid landscape covered in nothing but ice and snow. A sharp wind bit at his skin and turned it beet red. Zarek had stripped Baal's powers and begun his torture. Baal had been left with only a pair of jeans, a thin T-shirt and his boots. With no protection from the elements, he'd been instructed to start walking. He'd been told when he reached the other side, his sacrifice would be complete, and he would be set free. That is...if he made it.

While he was immortal, and therefore, wouldn't die from exposure, he would grow weak, and it was possible he'd never find his way out of the frozen tundra.

He focused and placed a picture of Ranata in his mind. She needed him, and fuck, if he didn't want her, as well. Failure wasn't an option. He wanted to keep his mind closed but had promised her he would be there if she needed him. If he couldn't be in person, at least, he could offer emotional support if she reached out.

Bracing against the wind, he began his trek through snow that was almost up to his knees in some places. Clouds darkened the sky, turning it to an angry gray. Baal had a difficult time distinguishing between blowing snow and what was falling from the sky. Either way, it didn't matter. It coated his hair, brows and lashes, turning them into a frozen mess. As his body shook uncontrollably, he became positive Zarek meant to end his existence. With no magic to aid him, he had no choice but to wander aimlessly in the hope he'd find the other side. If there even was one.

A howl sounded in the distance, followed by a growling that set his teeth on edge.

"Ah, hell." Would he have to defend himself against beasts as well as the elements? He wondered what else Zarek had in store for him. He reached out with his thoughts to touch Ranata. Maybe, that would help take his mind off his current misery.

When he connected, he received a rush of heat, but it was only temporary. *Sugar, everything okay?*

Yes. I'm talking to mother now. Thank you so much for giving me this gift.

Anything to make you happy. And he realized he meant every word. If she'd asked him for the moon, he'd figure out a way to put it on a silver chain and slip it around her neck. He loved her smile and intended to make her do it more often.

His next task was to get Raven back. As soon as Zarek was done making him into a snowman.

IRIS CLUTCHED RANATA'S HANDS. "I'm so proud of you. I understand the virus is under control now. You have saved your people from certain extinction."

Ranata shook her head. "All I did was provide a little blood."

"No. It was more than that. You never hesitated and stepped into this position though you had little knowledge of it. You accepted a man—no, a demon—as your mate without question."

"Well, I did question that one, and I'm still not sure I understand, but he's growing on me."

Her mother smiled, and her eyes sparkled. "You love him. I knew you would, and I knew he would protect you with his life."

"But will I ever have his heart?"

"You already do. Otherwise, he wouldn't be undergoing Zarek's torture right now." Iris plucked a grape off the tray in front of them and popped it into her mouth.

"What?" Ranata's blood ran cold. "What do you mean, torture?"

Iris's brows pinched down. "He didn't tell you. I might have known he would spare you his pain."

Ranata was suddenly overwhelmed with panic. "Mother, you must tell me."

"When he asked Zarek to grant us permission to be together, it came with a price."

Fear gripped her, followed by anger, and she was almost afraid to ask, but she needed to know. "What has Zarek done to my mate?"

Again, Iris smiled. "Ah, I recognize that passion in your eyes. You get it from me, and once it shows itself, there's no stopping you." She straightened. "Your mate was required to make a sacrifice for his request. He's been stripped of his magic and sent to a world full of snow and ice—something demons despise. He suffers greatly."

Rage filled her, and she jumped from her chair, knocking it over. "No. I can't allow him to suffer."

"Then you must confront the one who sent him there," Iris whispered.

Ranata balled her fists and clenched her jaw. "So I shall." She had no idea where Zarek was now, but maybe, if she yelled, he'd come to investigate ruckus. "Zarek!"

Nothing.

She opened her senses to Baal as she'd been taught and must have caught him off-guard. Pain filled her. Cold, biting pain. She gasped.

"Zarek, you will come to me, at once."

Finally, he appeared. "Are you done so soon?"

She focused on the one thing Kalin had taught her about magic.

Find it and take it. Make it yours to command. "I want my mate back. Now. I insist you stop this insanity."

The god crossed bulging arms over his chest and glared. "Your Highness. You should tread lightly while in my realm or feel my wrath."

"Bring it," she spat, not caring that he was far more powerful than her. Fear for Baal consumed her, and she would do anything to protect him.

Would you fight a god for him, daughter?

Yes.

Then do it.

It scarcely registered what her mother had whispered in her head. All Ranata could think about was the searing pain she'd felt when she'd connected to Baal, and she had to stop it. Now.

She focused her mind on the colors around her. Magic was thick in the air, and it snapped with power. She grabbed it and shielded herself and her mother against any retaliation Zarek might throw at them.

"Bring him back. Now." She felt the power growing inside her. Starting as a tiny ball of light, she nurtured and fed it until it flowed through her veins like lifeblood. It was part of her, and she was willing to use it. Even if it destroyed her.

"I will not ask again," she hissed.

"And I will not bend to the whims of a small female," Zarek replied.

Ranata raised her hands in front of her and sent a shockwave of energy straight at his chest. He flew back several yards and landed on his ass. A crowd gathered, and Zarek jumped to his feet.

A blast came back at her. She braced, but the shield held. She looked over at her mother who was grinning from ear to ear. Not even her hair had been blown out of place. Determined to get her mate back, Ranata called more power to her and threw it back at the god in a blaze of fire.

He shielded.

"I can hold out all day. Eventually, you'll tire and drop your guard," he growled.

"Never!" She had to find a way to win this.

"Then I will destroy the entire fae kingdom," he snapped.

No. They didn't deserve his wrath because of her. She was supposed to save them, not condemn them to death.

Don't let him threaten you, daughter. You have more power here than you'll ever get anywhere else. A queen puts her people above all others. Always.

She had to come up with a plan and quickly. Then it hit her, and she flashed a wide smile. "Maybe I will tire before you do, but..."

First, Kalin appeared at her side. Then one by one, the fae warriors. Over one-hundred men filtered in to stand behind her. She mentally reached for each and every one of them and connected. Together, they would siphon every drop of power in this place.

"You cannot beat us all. I may be new at this game, but I've learned enough to know I've just placed you in checkmate. Now... give me back my mate."

Zarek smiled, and Iris applauded, and now, Ranata was confused. Why did the god look pleased?

"You have passed your test and proved not only are you ready to fetch your sister, but you're ready to lead the fae," Zarek said. "You, my queen, have one huge set of balls."

"I don't understand." She looked to her mother, who had moved in next to her.

"Zarek would have given you your mate back when you asked, but he wanted to be sure you were ready for the challenges ahead of you. The best way he could figure to test you was to threaten the one thing most important to you. When you go for Raven, Lowan will seek vengeance, and he will try to destroy our people again. It is up to you to keep everyone safe," her mother replied.

"Lowan is only a demigod and less powerful than Zarek, and you proved not only can you handle the magic, but already, your people are devoted to you."

Ranata looked behind her and realized the magnitude of what had happened. "Holy shit. I really did this?"

Kalin beamed with pride. "Yes, you did, Your Highness. And with only one day of lessons. You opened a portal and brought your entire army to your side."

Wow, she had, hadn't she, but even she realized there was still much to learn. Later, though. "Fine, I passed your damn test. Now, where is Baal?"

Immediately, the demon was dropped at her feet. He rolled into a shivering ball. His skin held a bluish tint, as did his lips, and when she knelt to touch him, she found thick ice covered his lashes. She'd better take them out of here before her anger caused her to do something stupid. She looked up at Kalin.

"You're in charge until I return. Then, we go for Raven," she commanded.

"Yes, Your Highness."

She looked back at her mother, pain in her heart before she flashed herself and Baal to the one place she was sure they'd be left alone. His home in Hell. Hopefully, it would provide him a sense of comfort. She pulled the covers back on the bed then began to pull off his boots.

"S-sugar?"

"Hush, you foolish demon. You're home now." She continued undressing him until he was naked then she removed her own clothes and climbed in next to him. Pulling him close, she spooned his back and brought the covers up to their chins. Then she waited.

CHAPTER SEVENTEEN

BAAL ROLLED OVER, groaned then opened his eyes. "What the fuck?" He looked around and immediately recognized his bedroom in Hell. He sat up. Scratching his chin, he rewound his memories. The last thing he recalled, he was freezing his ass off in Zarek's torture chamber. Then a blurry image of Ranata standing over him surfaced. He sensed she was off in the other room, so he decided to take a quick detour to see Hades.

"What the hell happened?" he asked Hades. "I know I didn't spend a week in that shit hole, and something tells me my mate is behind it."

Hades looked up from his gardening, and Baal frowned.

"What? The Lord of the Underworld can't like plants?" He went back to pruning a bush full of red flowers. Their pungent aroma burned Baal's nose.

"Spill. I know you have the details."

Hades stood and stretched. "Fine. She fought with Zarek and won. Well, at least, proved she was capable of defending the fae."

The tic started in Baal's temple and only worsened as the god replayed the story of what had happened. He was going to put that female over his knee. "I need to go punish my mate," he growled and vanished.

He took himself back to the bedroom, threw on a pair of jeans then headed into the other room. Ranata stood in front of the window looking outside. He stormed across the room, surprised she never sensed he was coming.

Good.

When he reached her, he grabbed her by the waist, spun her to face him then pushed her against the glass, pinning her arms over her head.

"You will never, and I mean *ever*, place yourself in danger again," he commanded. Her eyes lit and went as wild as a feisty cat. Perfect, she was sexy as hell when pissed.

"You've no room to talk." She struggled to free herself, but he was having none of it. "How dare *you* place *yourself* in danger?"

"Let's get one thing straight. I'm all for equal rights, but if you think I will ever allow you to fight my battles then you've thought wrong," he replied.

He felt her reaching for his magic. No doubt, she intended to steal it to escape, but he blocked her.

The look of surprise on her face was priceless. "How?"

"I am the strongest demon in Hades' army. Why do you think he chose me as your mate? You can't best me, sugar. You can only take what I give you."

His little fae seethed and was currently weak as a mortal. He planned to take full advantage of the situation. He pressed against her and nipped at her bottom lip.

She tried to turn away, but he simply suckled on her neck.

"Damn you," she whispered, and when she turned to face him, he claimed her mouth. He swept his tongue in and tasted every inch of her. She melted into him, and he had to fight to keep from chuckling. He knew what she wanted and broke off the kiss with another nip to her swollen lips.

"When this started, I told you I could never give you my heart. It was broken long ago."

"Then why do you care what I do?" she asked, lifting her chin.

"Because somewhere along the line, I was blindsided. Some damn female wove my heart back together then stole it." He pressed his forehead to hers. "Damn it, woman. You know my past. Don't make history repeat itself. I love you, and I will tear the universe to shreds if anything happens to you."

"I... Did you just say you love me?" Her blue eyes widened, her nervousness evident as she nibbled her bottom lip. Had he fucked up by admitting his feelings? He'd been positive she felt the same way. The last time they were together he'd thought something had passed between them. No matter.

"I did. So, what of it?"

"I just wanted to make sure I'm not hallucinating." Her eyes became hooded. "Are you going to do something with me?"

He leaned in and nipped her earlobe. "Oh, am I ever."

She sucked in a breath. "I need..."

"I know." He needed her, as well, and planned to have her. Kissing her, he ran his hands down her arms and along the bottom of her breasts. He cupped the full mounds and rolled the nipples between his fingers.

She moaned, gripping the waistband of his jeans. "Too many clothes."

"I can fix that." He debated whether he should simply wish their clothes off or...

He grabbed the hem of the pink tank top she wore and ripped. Rose-tipped breasts greeted him. "Oh, yeah, that was much more satisfying than zapping them away."

He bent his head and latched onto a nipple while he snaked his hand into her panties. She was wet, and it was his turn to groan. He wanted to devour her, but first, he would bring her pleasure. He slipped one finger into her hot sex, then a second. She ran her hands through his hair and moved against him. He freed his fingers and spread her moisture across her clit.

"Oh, damn," she cried out.

Damn was right. He couldn't take any more. Her arousal filled his nostrils and thickened his cock to the point of painful. He pulled back and, with a quick jerk, had her panties off, along with her torn top. Her naked beauty stood before him like a goddess, begging to be worshipped.

He flicked his wrist, and his jeans disappeared, freeing his erection. A look of disappointment came over her.

"You screwed me out of stripping you." She stuck out her bottom lip.

"Oh, I'm going to screw you all right." He dropped to his knees, pulled her left leg over his shoulder and spread her tender, pink flesh. He ran his tongue over her clit.

"Christ." She tugged at his hair. "You keep that up, and I'll be coming in seconds."

Precisely what he'd intended. He showed no mercy. Sliding his hand up her thigh, he inserted two fingers, shoving them deep then pulling them out until he had a fast rhythm going. He continued laving his tongue across her clit, and it wasn't long before he was rewarded with her screaming in ecstasy. Not giving her a moment to regain her composure, he gently lowered her leg to the floor then rose. Pressing her against the window, he cupped his hands under her ass and lifted. She instinctively knew what he wanted and wrapped her long, slender legs around his waist. He reached down and guided his cock to her entrance.

With a quick thrust, he was deep inside her. He was home, and the demon inside him growled in contentment. She clawed at his back, and it only served to fuel the fire that burned inside him.

He groaned as he slid in and out of her tight sheath, and he swore he'd never tire of this woman. Gone were the days of jumping from bed to bed, and he realized that while he had indeed loved Beth, it had been nothing compared to what he felt for Ranata.

She tugged on his hair and pulled his mouth to hers. She was a needy wench, and he loved her even more for it. Her kiss burned with passion as her tongue caressed his. She pulled his bottom lip between her teeth and bit gently. It was enough to send his cock pumping his seed deep inside her.

She peppered kisses along his jaw and up to his ear. "I love you, too."

He grinned, and his cock hardened again. "Let's go back to bed. I plan to fuck you until you can't walk."

She smiled wide. "Let's go, big boy."

RANATA HID in the shadows beside Kalin and Baal while they watched Raven, who was followed by at least ten demons as she strolled through a shopping mall as though her life were perfectly normal. Baal had shrouded the three of them in magic so they couldn't be seen.

"We can take them, no problem," Ranata said.

Kalin nodded. "The rest of our warriors are reinforcing our shields back home. We have no idea how long before Lowan realizes she's gone, but when he does, there'll be hell to pay."

Baal rubbed his hands together. "I'd love a piece of that fucker."

She touched his shoulder. "We're not here to confront him." She realized he wanted revenge for what the demigod had put his sister through. She did, too, but not at the expense of lives and most certainly not her mate's. "Can you two take care of the demons? I'll grab Raven."

Baal feigned a yawn. "Those demons are dust under my boot. Nothing but a speck."

She tried not to roll her eyes. "I'm going in." The mall was deserted, except for her sister and the posse following her, so Ranata flashed into Raven's path.

Her sister's jaw dropped, and she glanced over her shoulder. "Ranata, what are you doing here?"

"I'm here to fetch you."

Raven's eyes narrowed. "Don't be stupid. And how the hell did you get here?"

"We need to go." No sooner had the words passed her lips than Baal and Kalin attacked. Fire came from nowhere, and she grabbed her sister by the arm. "We're leaving."

She flashed back to the castle and to the room they'd prepared for Raven.

"How did you do that? Where are we?" Raven looked like a scared little girl, and all Ranata wanted to do was pull her sister into her arms and promise everything would be okay.

Sugar, you know what has to be done.

She's my sister.

I know, but it's for the safety of both of you, as well as all the fae.

I'm going. She flashed then stood outside a force field that surrounded the room. Raven tried to walk toward her but bumped into the shields.

"What the...?" She placed her hands on the invisible wall. Panic etched heavy lines across her face. "Ranata, let me out!"

"I'm sorry. This is for your protection, and that of our people."

"No. You don't understand. He will kill you. He's a monster." She dropped to her knees and sobbed.

Ranata's heart shattered, and she fought back her own tears.

"Raven, I have so much to tell you." She joined her sister on the floor and placed a hand on the force field Kalin and Baal had set up around the room. Hopefully, Lowan would be unable to detect Raven, and it would give them time to figure out if he had a tracking spell on her, or something worse.

"You're not safe. Once he knows I'm gone, he will hunt me down and punish us both. Please, if you love me, let me go."

"It's because I love you that you'll stay. We have people here, Raven. I met mother while you were away."

"Momma?" Raven was suddenly like a small child, and Ranata wished she could reach in and pull her sister tightly to her.

"Yes. Let me tell you about her. She was a brave, wondrous woman, and she was a queen." Her tears stung her cheeks. She'd had so little time with her mother. Not even the allotted hour because of Zarek and his games. She made a mental note to corner the god and demand a do-over.

"A queen? Now, you're telling tales." Raven sniffed.

Ranata couldn't help a soft chuckle. Her life indeed seemed like a fairytale. Now she was the queen of the fae, and her Prince Charming was a devilishly handsome demon. How had she gone from serving drunks in a remote dive bar to this? She had to pinch herself to make sure it wasn't a dream. She found the telepathic link to the cook and asked for a tray of food and drink to be brought to them. She and Raven had a lot to catch up on.

BAAL HELD Ranata in his arms, both of them still glowing after a long session of lovemaking. "Woman, if you insist on rubbing your foot up and down my leg, I'll be forced to take you again."

She nuzzled his neck. "Is that a threat?"

"A promise."

"Then I shall keep at it."

"You're insatiable," he laughed.

She bit his shoulder. "I am, but only when it comes to you." She sighed. "I can't believe how things have changed between us." She sat up, her eyes wide and staring right at him. "You promise you'll never leave?"

He understood where her fear came from. Everyone she'd ever loved had left her, and even he, in the beginning, had vowed never to give her his heart. What a damn fool he'd been, but he'd only been trying to protect himself. He stroked her cheek. "All the demons of Hell could never take me away from you. You're stuck with me." To prove his point, he opened up and let his emotions flow into her. "You own my heart now. Take care of it."

She smiled and snuggled back into him. "I will cherish it forever. So, what happens next?"

"Aidyn has called a meeting later this week with all the factions. Lileta and Caleb will attend for the Draki. Katie, Seth's mate, will represent the gods, even though she was sworn not to interfere. You will be there for the fae, and I for the Kothar race. I think you should take Kalin with you," he urged.

"I agree. He's anxious to enter the fight. Do you think Lowan will ever be destroyed?" She had switched to tracing circles on his chest.

"Yes. I have to believe he will. Though, now, I wonder about this other that Hades mentioned." He kissed the top of her head. "Once this is over and things are back to normal, would you consider maybe part-time residence at my home in Hell?"

She lifted her head. "I'd love that. I kinda like that place." Her brows furrowed. "What about the casino?"

"I don't need to be there all the time now. I have good managers. Besides, it's not a place to raise children."

"Children? I hadn't thought about that." Her face became panic stricken. "Oh, Baal. I want children, but now is not the time, and we've used no protection."

"Easy. Unlike other immortals, I can make myself sterile or fertile at will. When we are ready for children, we'll discuss it further."

"Well, isn't that convenient," she smiled.

"Can be."

She tucked back into him. "Do you think Raven will be safe? She seems pretty accepting of who she is."

Baal snorted. He'd been down to pay a visit with Raven, and she'd been conversing with Kalin—or rather, the fae commander had been busy telling her how things were going to be. "I'm sure Kalin will see to her safety."

Ranata chuckled. "I've noticed he is rather bossy with her, but he's helped us connect using our telepathic link. I'm grateful to him for that. When do you think it will be safe to let her out?"

"I'm leaving that one up to Kalin. Soon, I'd think, since the lab rats have cleared her of any tracking devices."

She slapped him on the arm. "Those lab rats are my friends."

He rolled her onto her back and poised himself over her.

She squealed.

"I love you, sugar. If they're important to you, then they're important to me." He gazed into her blue depths. "You remember the demon from the night I rescued you?"

Her pupils dilated. "Yes."

"Will you still love me if I tell you that was me? I shifted so I could get in there and make them think I was the one they were sacrificing you to."

Her features softened. "You did that for me?" She palmed his cheek. "I will love you no matter what."

"And I will do whatever it takes to protect you. Always." He slanted his mouth over hers and was about to nestle his cock in her warm depths when a siren sounded, indicating intruders had broken through their barriers. Baal leapt from the bed and dressed in seconds, taking a dagger in each hand. He looked back at his mate.

"Dress and arm yourself, but do not leave this room unless I give you the all clear."

He flashed.

CHAPTER EIGHTEEN

RANATA QUICKLY DRESSED and grabbed the weapons Kalin had made for her.

Baal, what the hell is going on?

A couple of Lowan's minions have managed to get in. Nothing to worry about. They've been dispatched, but stay put. I've placed guards around you.

She paced their bedroom. *How did they get in?*

Investigating that now.

She continued her pacing then panic set in again. "Shit."

Raven? Are you okay?

She chewed her lip, waiting for an answer, but seconds ticked by and nothing. "Fuck this. I'm not hiding in my room." She flashed to the lower level where Raven was staying and crossed the room.

"Raven?"

"Well, Your Highness. You arrived quicker than I'd hoped."

Ranata spun around and found Heremon with a knife to her sister's throat. "What the hell?" She'd known she didn't like that fae.

"Don't even think to call for help. I'll know, and I'll take her head off," Heremon growled.

Did she dare contact Baal? What if Heremon wasn't bluffing? She couldn't take that chance with her sister's life. "What do you want?"

"First thing. Drop that dagger and kick it toward me," he commanded.

She obeyed without hesitation.

"Good. Now, the three of us are leaving. Lowan wants his bitch back, and you're going to sweeten the pot."

"No. Take me, but leave Ranata here. I'll go willingly," Raven said.

"Sorry, not part of my plan," the fae replied.

"What makes you think you can get away from here with both of us?" Ranata inquired. She needed to think fast. She had no idea how skilled Heremon was, but she had to assume, since he was much older than her and born fae, he would be more powerful. Still, if she let him take her and Raven out of here, they might never survive. The thought of losing her sister again and maybe never seeing Baal sat like lead in her gut.

A portal opened across the room. Heremon shoved Raven forward. "You first, Your Highness." He jerked his head at Ranata.

"You kill her, and Lowan will surely have your head." Ranata stood her ground, hoping to buy some time and searched for the magic belonging to her mate. Heremon shifted his weight. Her statement succeeded in making him nervous.

"Lowan will thank me for taking out the bitch. He's not fond of those who betray him." He pressed the blade against Raven's skin until blood trickled down her neck. If he'd meant to get a reaction from either woman, he'd failed. Ranata kept her cool while fighting an internal battle. She realized she had no clue how to get her sister away from harm without endangering Raven further.

An idea came to her. "Heremon. What has Lowan offered you? Money? Power? I will give you more." She opened herself to Baal and focused on the scene in front of her. Without words, she let her fear pour from her and hoped he would understand they were in trouble. If Heremon sensed her fear, he would think nothing of it.

Heremon laughed. "I want your kingdom, Your Highness. Lowan has promised it to me, and unfortunately, your death and that of your sister must come to pass. You're the last heirs, so with you gone, I can finally rule."

She fisted her hands. "You were responsible for killing my mother!"

"I let his goons in, but I took her life myself. She never saw it coming." He cackled like an old woman, and Ranata's temper flared. She wanted the man dead but wasn't sure she could end a life.

He'll die by my hand, sugar. Get ready to run.

Baal had understood her message and relief swept over her. She glanced out of the corner of her eye, waiting to see him appear. Then, suddenly, Heremon shoved Raven away from him and grabbed at his throat. It was then Baal, Kalin and several others appeared. Baal stormed forward and looked every bit the pissed off warrior.

"Take Raven, and go with Kalin," Baal commanded. "You don't need to witness what I'm going to do to this scumbag."

She grabbed Raven and pulled her sister into an embrace. "You're still bleeding."

"Don't worry. We have healers standing by, Your Highness. Hurry," Kalin urged and scooped Raven into his arms before leading Ranata through another portal he'd opened. When they came out the other side, the opening snapped shut behind them.

"Where are we?" she asked, but the realization hit that the corridors looked familiar. "This is where I was brought when Baal rescued me." She recognized Cassie running toward them.

"Quick, bring her in here." The guardian ushered them into a room and pointed to the couch. "Put her there."

Kalin gently laid Raven down and stepped aside, allowing room for Cassie to move in. She touched Raven's wound. "I'm going to fix you right up." She smiled. "Luckily, it's not deep and your blood loss is minimal." As soon as the words passed her lips, she pulled her hand away. "There, all done."

Ranata slipped in next to her sister, who was now sitting up. "How do you feel?"

"Fine, but where are we? He's going to keep looking for me until he finds me." Panic laced Raven's voice.

"He won't find you here."

Ranata stood and ran into Baal's arms. "Oh, thank god, you're safe." She leaned back and stared into his eyes. "I was afraid to communicate with you and wasn't sure you'd get my message."

"Oh, I got it. You don't have to worry about Heremon ever again." He squeezed her to him. "You did good today. Don't ever worry about getting blood on your hands. I'll take care of the messy stuff." He bent down and planted a kiss on her lips.

"Thank you. Now, what? Where are the rest of the fae?" She was concerned Lowan would manage to spread his taint among them again.

"All here for now. Kalin and I will question everyone to make sure Heremon didn't have more inside help. Once everyone is cleared, Kalin has another hiding place ready for you."

She rested her head on his chest and listened to his beating heart. "When this is over, can we take a honeymoon like a real couple?"

He kissed the top of her head. "I'll take you anywhere you want to go. The world is your playground."

"I can't wait." She tipped her head back. "Whatever we have to do, let's end this mess and send Lowan and his minions back to Hell. I'm anxious to have some alone time with you."

"It will be done." He leaned in and pressed his lips to her ear. "When things calm, you will have your white dress and your wedding day. Anything you desire will be yours."

Tears stung her eyes, and she squeezed him tighter. "I'm the luckiest woman in the world." The gods really did know what they were doing.

YOU GO FOR THE GIRL, and get her out of here. I'll deal with the demon. Burning him to a crisp will be entertaining. Jax's laugh still rang in Lucan's head as he ran to the building where Willow was being held.

Magic clung to the surface of the stone structure, but it wasn't as powerful as the barrier Jax had brought down outside. Lucan shifted and slid through a tiny opening. Once on the other side, he returned to human form and opened his senses.

Willow was locked in a cell at the end of the corridor.

He ran, a dagger clutched in his hand and his senses on high alert. Who knew what kind of fucked-up mess he'd run into? As he passed several holding cells, he noticed other demons locked away. Apparently, this was Lowan's prison.

He stopped in front of Willow's cell and peeked inside. A frail-looking female sat curled up in a corner of the room. Her pale skin and light hair looked like what he'd seen in the demon's mind.

"Willow?"

She lifted her head. "Are you here to torture me again? Simply kill me, and be done with it."

He tested the door. Locked. "Fuck it." He flashed inside. "I'm here to take you home."

Hope flashed in her eyes then quickly turned to anger. "Don't mock me."

"I'm not." He moved toward her. Already, the magic surrounding them shifted. Someone, most likely Lowan, knew there was a breach and was working to fix it. Lucan scooped her off the floor, noting how she weighed next to nothing. The poor thing had been starved. While fae were immortal, they still required some nourishment to remain strong.

"Don't fear. I'm a guardian and here on behalf of your brother." *Well sorta.*

She looked up at him and gave him a weak smile. "You're Lucan, are you not?"

He was surprised since he'd never met Willow. She was much younger than Chaval. They'd been grown by the time she'd been born. "Yes. How did you know?"

"Sabin has told me about you." She gasped. "You must save her, too."

"She's here?" He wondered why she hadn't tried to pry open his mind. "What is she? Who is she?" There was no time for answers. The corridors became flooded with demons, and he had to leave now. "We've gotta go."

He flashed back to the upper level where Jax waited with an open portal.

"Hurry. Here they come," the Draki yelled. Lucan glanced quickly behind him and witnessed hundreds of demons descending upon them. He ran through the portal with Jax on his tail. It slammed shut just in a nick of time. He headed straight for the infirmary of their compound. *Baal, Marcus. I have Willow with me.* He placed her on a bed, and Baal, Marcus and Aidyn stormed through the door.

"How is she?" Aidyn asked, stepping up beside them.

She turned to look at him. "My lord, you have not changed since I was a little girl. I am sorry about your mother."

Aidyn raised a brow. "You heard about her death?"

She nodded. "Lowan was always free with the news of the faction. He thought it would break our spirits more by causing us to miss our families." She looked at Lucan. "You must go back for Sabin."

Baal and Aidyn gave him a questioning look. He wasn't ready to admit he'd been having conversations with the mysterious woman.

"Who is she?" Lucan shook his head. "I don't think there's any going back there. They'll be expecting us this time."

She pushed herself to sitting. "You must, before he kills her. Lowan pledged that his sister would die on her three-hundredth birthday."

"What?" the four men chimed in unison. Aidyn held up his hand.

"Are you saying this Sabin is Lowan's sister?"

Lucan ran his hands through his hair. *Son of a bitch! I knew she was the devil herself.* "No fucking way I'm going to risk my neck to save that piece of shit's sister. Why would you even suggest it?" he growled.

Willow touched Lucan on the arm. "You must. She is your mate."

ABOUT THE AUTHOR

Award winning and bestselling author Valerie Twombly grew up watching Dark Shadows over her mother's shoulder, and from there her love of the fanged creatures blossomed. Today, Valerie has decided to take her darker, sensual side and put it to paper. When she is not busy creating a world full of steamy, hot men and strong, seductive women, she juggles her time between a full-time job, hubby and her German shepherd dog, in Northern IL. Valerie is a member of Romance Writers of America and Fantasy, Futuristic and Paranormal Romance Writers.

Sign up for Valerie's newsletter and be the first to hear about new releases, receive special excerpts and exclusive contests. http://valerietwombly.com/newsletter-sign/

Follow Valerie
www.valerietwombly.com

ALSO BY VALERIE TWOMBLY

Visit ValerieTwombly.Com

Guardians Series

Vampire's Mate Book 1

Dragon's Fate Book 2

Vampire's Kiss Book 3

Demon's Destiny Book 4

Hades Book 5

Vampire's Queen Book 6

Vampire's Desire Book 7

Eternally Mated Series

An Angel's Torment Prequel

Fall Into Darkness Book 1

Veiled In Darkness Book 2

Bound By Darkness Book 3

Unleash The Darkness Book 4

Surrender To Darkness Book 5

Tempted By Darkness Book 6

Sparks Of Desire Series

His Burning Desire

Rescue Me

Finding Hope

Demonic Desires Series

Taken By Desire Book 1

Taken By Storm Book 2
Jinn's Seductions Series
Spanish Nights
Sultry Nights
Beyond The Mist Series
Passion Awakened (Beyond The Mist)